# GRAND REAPER
## The Soul Snatcher

Linda Spence Howard

Wider Perspectives Publishing ∞ Hampton Roads, Va. ∞ 2021

Wider Perspectives Publishing
Copyright © Linda Spence Howard, 2021, Portsmouth, Va
ISBN: 978-1-952773-32-7

## about your author Linda Spence Howard

Linda Spence Howard is currently 41 years old. She was born to the late Mr. & Mrs. Luemel and Hattie Howard in Portsmouth, Virginia, where she was raised in the Prentice Park and Ida Barbour neighborhoods. She later moved to Academy Park where she attended Woodrow Wilson High School. Linda has four beautiful daughters, all born and raised in Portsmouth. Linda started her writing career in 2018, this will be her first published novel.

# Contents

chapters

# Chapter 1

There was a man named Mr. Benjamin Jackson, who lived in a town called Hollowfield, Virginia. This town was very small; the kind where everyone knew everyone. Benjamin Jackson worked as a groundskeeper in a cemetery. One day Mr. Jackson was working late into the afternoon when he heard strange sounds. He got a little closer to the sounds as they started to get louder and louder. He noticed that there were two teenage boys horseplaying around; The Matthew brothers. Ethan and Logan were always in and out of trouble with the law. Mr. Jackson walked over and asked the two young gentlemen what they were doing in the cemetery so late. They looked back at Mr. Jackson and started to laugh… one of the Matthew brothers yelled out, "Hey, you don't belong here either old man!"

Linda Spence Howard

Mr. Jackson turned and looked back as he replied, "Well I need you two boys to get up and get out of here, please. Now let me on with my day. I don't want any trouble."

The Matthew boys just went right on laughing at Mr. Jackson as he turned and started to walk away. Suddenly Logan picked up an iron pipe as he ran behind Mr. Jackson and hit him over the head with it. Ethan turned around and looked at Logan with a frightened look on his face. "Man what did you do? How hard did you hit him?" Ethan ran to where Logan stood over Mr. Jackson. He tried to turn Mr. Jackson over but the man didn't move at all. "I don't think he's alive, Logan, What did you do?"

Logan towered over and, with the iron pole, started to nudge him on his side. Mr. Jackson still didn't move. Logan dropped the pipe out of his hand and started to step back. Logan turned and looked over at Ethan and said, "I think we just killed the old man."

Ethan looked at his brother with a frown on his face., "We... What you mean we? Naw!... you mean, you killed the old man. I didn't have that iron pipe in my hand, this is all your doing."

As Logan looked up he said, "We are in this together... if I go down, you're going down, too. So now... What are we going to do? We can't tell no one or they are going to put us in jail.

Logan's hands and forehead had begun to sweat as he paced back and forth. Ethan turned and looked over his shoulder, back at his brother in a strange way. "Look! ... I think you need to calm the hell down! So we can figure out what the hell to do with this body."

Logan hollered out, "I have an idea, let's dig a hole and put him in it."

Ethan turned around and looked at his brother up and down, "So you're telling me... that if we dig a hole, no one will come looking for this old man... not even down to the police?

That's the best idea you have come up with all night?!" Ethan looked back over at Logan with a surprised look – as if he knew this couldn't ever work.

Logan turned around and looked over at Ethan and hollered out, "Yes, so start digging dammit! Look, I'm already nervous, so please dig!" So the Matthew brothers began to dig a large hole so they could put Benjamin Jackson's body in it. As they threw Mr. Jackson into the six foot grave, they did not realize that he was still breathing, merely unconscious. They tried to cover the hole, as tightly as they could get it.

The more dirt they packed on it, the more it seemed like the hole kept getting bigger and bigger. Ethan looked down at the ground and noticed that Mr. Jackson's name tag had fallen off of his shirt. He hurriedly bent down and grabbed it off the ground, then slowly put it into his packet.

Logan looked up in time to see the gesture and asked, "what was that you just put in your pocket?"

As Ethan turned around he replied "Nothing! Let's finish packing the dirt so we can get out of here." Ethan looked over at Logan and said, "We can not tell no one what happened tonight, Okay? If anyone asks, we haven't seen this old man. The answer is 'no.' Do you understand Logan?" As Logan stood frozen, looking down at the grave, starting to stare. Ethan dropped the shovel and grabbed his brother by the arm.

He took Logan by the shoulder and started to shake him. "Dammit Logan, you can't get scared on me now! We are in this together," He took the palm of his hand and came across Logan's face, "What the hell is wrong with you?! Snap out of it. Now look; Like I said, we have to stay together so that way no one or the police will get any suspicions, but you have to stay calm, cool and positive about this whole thing... You got that?"

*Linda Spence Howard*

The more Logan looked at the grave, the more he started to tense up, "Man I can't do this mess... I can't go to jail! Ethan turned around and just stared, then, "What?! What the hell you mean, 'you can't do this.'? You're the one that hit the old man over the head. And now you want to say you can't do this! The devil is a liar. You will not leave me out here high and dry, little brother. Like I said, like it or not, we are in this together or you will be down there with that old bastard! Now quit playing and help me patch up this damn hole."

As they finished covering up the hole a police car rode by the cemetery and flashed the big spot light from the side. The Matthew brothers looked up and saw the police car. Logan and Ethan dove into the grave where Mr. Jackson was. Logan turned over he saw the face of Mr. Benjamin Jackson looking right up at him. Logan turned his head and looked right at Ethan, "Hell no! We can't stay in this big grave with no dead man! The police already knows what we've done."

Ethan turned his head slowly around and said in a low tone, "If you wouldn't have never hit the old man we wouldn't be in this mess. But oh no! Mr. Logan just gotta have it his way or no way."

As they laid there for a while in the dark grave Mr. Jackson's leg started to jerk back and forward, both of the Matthew boys looked down and immediately climbed out.

As they finished putting the last patch of dirt on the body of Mr. Benjamin Jackson they turned to look at one another and they swore to never tell a living soul what happened on that September evening.

# Chapter 2

That night, Ethan and Logan had gone to bed thinking about the old man that they had put in the ground early that day. Logan could not sleep. He tossed and turned as he lifted his head up and looked over at Ethan to see him where he was asleep. "Ethan!" Logan called out to him.

Ethan opened his eyes, "What?"

"Are you sleep?"

"No I'm not, how can I be asleep if you're calling me, Logan?"

Logan sat up on the bed, still looking at Ethan's directions, "What are we going to do about the old man that we just killed?"

Linda Spence Howard

As Ethan turned over and set up on his bed he shot back, "We?! What the hell you mean we?! I have already told you over and over again. I didn't kill the old bastard, you did. So stop saying we!"

Logan's head dropped as he looked back up at Ethan. "But I thought that you were going to help me and try to figure this thing out. And besides you are in it – because you help me dig the hole, remember brother Ethan." Suddenly, a soft knock hit the front door.

Both of the Matthew brothers looked at one another. Well, Who could that be at this time of the night. and what do they want? As they both got up to see who was at the front door. The sound got louder and louder. Then, when they got close to the door, the noise stopped. Just when Logan began to reach for the door handle a gust of wind came blowing through. "Did you feel that?" Logan asked Ethan with a look upon his face as if he had seen a ghost.

Ethan replied, "No, I didn't feel anything. And quit playing around and open up the door."

So when Logan open up the front door, there was no one standing there – just the pitch black darkness. The moon shone, and somewhere a wolf howled in the night, but the brothers couldn't believe what they saw – which was nothing. It seemed all there was to do was look at each other with their wide-open mouths.

Ethan came around Logan to shut the door, but suddenly a black dust came blowing in Ethan's face on a strong wind. As they both tried to shut the front door the wind was so heavy and strong, that they could not close it. Ethan fell to the floor while Logan was still trying to close the door. The door would not shut.

"Ethan," Logan cried out, "I can't hold this door any longer!" When he saw that Ethan was on the floor, "this is no damn time to be playing on the floor Ethan! Get up and help me."

Ethan pulled himself up, jumping to his feet, and started to help Logan with the door. Ethan looked up at Logan and asked, "What the hell was that? That hit me in my face. I don't know, but there is something strange going on here."

As they both pushed the door tight a howling sound whispered from all around the room saying , "I want my revenge... I want your soul." The Matthew brothers stopped and looked all around the room, but didn't see anyone there.

Logan started to run and reach for his gun, but the black fog became so dark so and heavy that he could not see a thing. The black gusts of wind swirled all round the Matthew brothers. They tried to fall close to the floor so they can crawl their way out of the darkening winds. Logan reached out his hand for Ethan, but all he felt was a hard heavy boot. Logan called out, "Ethan! Where are you bro?! Speak to me! Hold out your hand so I can grab it!" However, the more he tried to reach out to grab his brother's hand, the more he just felt the heavy big boot. Logan quickly snatched his hand away. As the gust of wind began to get thicker and heavier, Logan and Ethan began to gag – they were losing their breath. Then Mr. Benjamin Jackson appeared in his hat and black rain boots.

The Matthew brothers pretended to play dead, unmoving, as the heavy gust of wind and cloud slowly started to disappear, revealing Mr. Jackson's a black overalls suit. Ethan and Logan slowly opened their eyes to look around, wondering where the gusts of wind had gone. As they got up and looked up they saw all of their pictures turn upside down.

They turned and looked at one another and knew that they had seen the old man – Mr. Benjamin Jackson. As the sun began to rise for that morning the Matthew brothers went to the window to look out to see if the town still looked the same. Ethan had started to wonder if that was the old man spirit, or was that their mind

*Linda Spence Howard*

playing tricks on them. "Well, I think we need to get ready for school." Ethan said. He turned toward Logan, "Remember, we can't tell no one what happened the other night, Okay!"

Logan nodded his head.

As he was walking up the stairs Ethan remembered that he had Mr. Jackson's name still in his pocket. As he went through his pocket then pulled out the name tag his eyes opened up very wide and bright as he thought, 'Maybe that's what he wants ... his name tag. Or is it that he came to warn us and remind us of what we did to him.' The more he thought about it the more he was getting paranoid.

# Chapter 3

As Ethan ran upstairs to get ready for school he stopped in the hallway. Just then he started to feel a cool breeze. As he walked into his room the breeze started to get even colder. Ethan stopped once more, then he turned around and called for Logan. Logan yelled out, "Yes, what is it?"

"I wanted to know if you turned on the air."

Logan looked up with a strange look upon his face. "No! why the hell would I turn on the A.C.? Have you been drinking again Ethan?"

Ethan came into Logan's room and stood in the doorway. "No, I have not been drinking!" It's cold as hell in this house. You

*Linda Spence Howard*

don't feel that cool breeze that's coming from the hallway?" As Logan went to step out of his room to try to feel the cool breeze that Ethan was feeling it had vanished.

"No, I don't... and quit playing around and let's get ready for school. I can't wait until June gets here so I can tell those teachers where to go at." As they both headed out of the door Ethan remembered the name tag that was on the coffee table. When he ran back in the house to grab it the door slammed and locked. Ethan banged and kicked as hard as he could on the front door. Ethan began yelling out. "Help me! Open the door, Logan!"

Logan tried to push and kick the front door in, but the door would not open. Then, all of the sudden another gust of wind started to blow even harder knocking leaves and tree branches all over the front yard. Logan ran to the other side of the house and tried to open the back door, but it was also stuck. He tried to push the door with his shoulder over and over again. Finally, the door opened, and he rushed in running into the living room. The shadow of Mr, Benjamin Jackson was standing in the middle of the floor.

Logan froze in his tracks and stared as if he saw a ghost. The more he looked at the shadow, the more be believed his eyes were deceiving him. The shadow of Mr. Benjamin Jackson started to swirl in circles around the Matthew brothers. Ethan looked down at his gold necklace with its design of the cross of Jesus,. He took off the necklace and put it in his hand, then he held it up in the air and pointed it right at the shadow of Benjamin Jackson. The black shadow began to holler and cry out as it swirled out into thin air. Logan and Ethan both covered their faces. until the black dust cleared the room. Ethan looked up at Logan and said, "Well, at least we know what and how to kill it with now," a little grin on his face.

Logan looked up at the ceiling then looked back down and began to laugh as if he was stung from what he had seen. Logan looked at Ethan in a weird way. "And may I ask, what the hell is so funny?"

Logan replied, looking at Ethan as if he could strangle him, "We missed a whole day of school messing around with a stupid dusty ghost that we are not sure of... what or who it is. And you really don't think that's funny? Well, I think it's hilarious."

Ethan got up off the floor and looked at Logan and said, "You a damn fool! you know that? We are in this big ass house and we get attacked by an unwanted ghost or spirit... or whatever you want to call it. If you wouldn't have hit the old man over the head maybe we wouldn't be in this mess.

Logan turned around and asked, "How do you know that is the old man? What do you know, Ethan?" As Ethan started to walk away Logan came behind him and asked again, "Ethan, I have asked you a question: How do you know that this thing or ghost is that old man?"

Ethan looked straight ahead at the coffee table. then back at Logan. Logan turned around and saw the name tag on the table... As he walked over to the coffee table and picked up the name tag he saw the name of Mr. Benjamin Jackson. "You lied to me; I asked you what was that you had put in your pocket, And you told me 'nothing.' You knew the whole entire time who this man was, and you didn't say a word. This ghost or spirit wants revenge because of what we have done."

Ethan's eyes had started to squint, "What do you mean 'We'? I have already told you once that I didn't have a thing to do with this. This is all you baby boy. So you're gonna to have to do this all by yourself."

Logan laughed again, "You keep forgetting pretty boy Ricky, you help me dig the hole, so if I go down, oh for sure you're going down! You got that?"

Ethan stepped back and looked at him with an unpleasant look, "Yeah I got it."

Logan took a deep breath in, "Well, since we aren't going to school we might as well clean up this mess that the unwanted guest made."

As they began to clean up the house, they started to see a bit of blood that had dripped on the floor. Logan stopped sweeping and looked up at the ceiling, and as he did, he saw a big black shadow with blood dripping from it. Logan slowly walked over to Ethan, still looking up at the ceiling, and he tapped Ethan on the shoulder. He pointed up. Now they both saw the black shadow covered with deep red blood.

# Chapter 4

"Oh my Lord!" Ethan hollered out as he took in what was on the ceiling. They both started to back away when the blood on the ceiling started to drip slowly down. As more and more blood drooped and then splashed down from the ceiling it seemed to turn into acid. Ethan began to pushed on Logan to hurry him into the kitchen, then they both tried to run for the back door. The black shadow, separating from the ceiling of the one room, moved quickly towards the Matthew brothers in the kitchen.

Sliding down the walls Mr. Benjamin Jackson started to appear from the shadow. Mr. Jackson started out walking very slowly with blood dripping off of his hollow form. As if still made of shadow he sounded distant when he yelled out, "I want my revenge! I want your soul..."

Linda Spence Howard

Ethan grabbed for his cross, but the shadow knocked it out of his hand and it slid away. Finally seeming material the vision of Mr. Jackson picked Ethan up by the neck and started to squeeze tightly. Logan ran towards the black shadowy man, but with one hollow hand it smacked Logan dead to the floor. Ethan gasped out, "Logan get the cross! Point it at the shadow." Logan crawled toward the cross, grasped it, and pointed it at the black shadow of Mr. Benjamin Jackson. However, this time it didn't work. The shadow had become stronger.

The shadow had begun to open his mouth right in front of Ethan's face. It began to squeal and holler loudly with suction noise as if it could draw the breath right out of Ethan's mouth. Logan rolled over and tried to point the cross at it again. From the cross came a light that filled up the room as he pointed at the shadow once more. The shadow then did begin to feel the heat from the cross, and soon the shadow seemed to melt into liquid.

It still had a tight grip on Ethan's his throat, however, as its darkness slowly ran down it's own arms and feet. Ethan lowered to the floor by the time the shadow had disappeared into thin air. Ethan put his own hand around his throat, rubbing it over and over again.

Logan asked, "Hey man are you Okay?"

Ethan looked up at his brother, "Yeah I think so. Why the hell this thing keeps on attacking us? What does it want?"

Logan had got up off the floor and looked squarely at Ethan and said, "Didn't you hear what that spirit said he wanted from us? He wants revenge, and he wants our souls."

Ethan had stopped rubbing his throat to declare, "The hell he does! I'm not giving this ghost my spirit, soul or any part of my body. He is just going to have to kill me before I give him anything that belongs to me!"

Logan looked at him and started to shake his head, "... and that's what the hell he is going to do, is kill you!  If you don't come up with a plan, Ethan.  You think this is all fun and games?  Well, this is life we are talking about here!"

Ethan straightened up and met his brother's look. "Logan, I told you before, I'm not doing it.  This is all your fault!  If you wouldn't have gotten us in this mess. We wouldn't be dealing with a ... whatever you want to call it.

Logan returned with, "Okay let's not argue with each other right now.  We have a ghost to hurt down and kill... before it kills us.  Now, are you going to help me or not, Ethan?  It's your call, either you help track down this ghost or spirit or we both die.

# Chapter 5

Ethan stared intensely at the cross Logan still had it in his hand. As he went to hold out his hand and reach for it, Ethan looked up at Logan and said, "I think we need a couple more of these golden crosses. It really will come in handy just in case if the ghost or spirit should ever come back."

Logan looked up and just started to stare, "What are we going to do if this cross doesn't work? How are we supposed to get rid of this thing? I mean this thing or ghost has really gotten stronger, you saw the way he had you up in the air. My God ... this thing really wants us dead."

Logan just held his head down shaking it from side to side. Then all of a sudden a knock came upon the front door. It was a tall man with a blue hooded sweatshirt on with his back turned to the road. "Did you hear that?!" as Ethan held his head up and stared at

Logan. Logan looked back at him, then started to look all around the room.

"No! I didn't ... shhh!"

Ethan put one finger over his mouth. The knock cam again and started to get loud. "Hey is anyone there? Are you Okay?" The Matthew brothers both ran to the door. They opened the door and they saw Mr. Haywood standing there with his old sagging, wrinkly face.

"Hey, I thought I would stop by and check on you guy. I haven't seen you in a while. Is everything Okay? Mr. Haywood went to turn around and lift up his head, as the shadow slowly moved from behind him.

Logan looked at Ethan and then looked back at Mr. Haywood, "Yes. We're Okay, we just have some family issues going on, but if we need anything we know where to find you." Mr. Haywood just smiled and looked at the Matthew brothers.

"Well I just wanted to make sure that you guys are Okay." As he went to step off the front porch the cool breeze hit Logan and Ethan in their face.

"Wow! Did you feel that?" As Ethan turns and asks Logan he was still holding on to his cold wet face. This time Logan did feel the cool wet breeze on his face. All he could do was hold his hand up against his face and stare.

As both went back into the house. Ethan ran up stairs and started to search for his jewelry box. Soon he pulled out an old black box, that had silver beads wrapped around the edges with old spider webs covering it front and back. He quickly opened up the box to look for any type of cross. However, all he had were some old silver and gold rings.

"Dag!" as he thought to himself. 'I know I had to have some more crosses around here somewhere, but where?' As he kept thinking about those crosses. Logan started to yell from the bottom of the stairs. "Hey man, what are you up there doing? What's taking you so long? Come on we still have to clean up this mess down here. Hey! Ethan do you hear me?"

As Ethan came running out of the room, "Yeah I hear you, and quit yelling like your damn mind has gone bad. I'm up here trying to find some more crosses, if you don't mind, so we can get rid of this unwanted ghost or spirit. Just of matter of fact, why don't you come up here and help me find them?"

Logan started up the stairs to help Ethan find the cross. "Hey! Do you think that this ghost or whatever this thing is – is it going to kill us?" Logan turns and asks Ethan.

Ethan stops and looks up at him, "Not if we get it first."

"Yeah I hope so, because I'm really getting tired of this damn ghost. You know we haven't slept in three nights since this happened. Ethan I really think we need to tell someone what really went on the other night."

Ethan stops once more and turns his head around. "Yeah, you are crazy, and get us thrown in jail for some that you done."

Logan leaned his head over, "Oh my god! there you go again with this mess: Yes I killed the man. There! Are you happy now!? I said it. Now, let's move the hell on, so we won't die tonight."

# Chapter 6

Later, that night, as they both got ready for bed. Logan looked over at Ethan and said, "Hey, I'm sorry for early today when I yell at you."

Ethan turned his head and looked back at him and said, It's Okay, you were just upset. Now get some sleep, we can't afford any no more days out of school."

The next morning as the Matthew brothers got up for school they noticed that the floor was covered with blood. Yet upon second look the blood had disappeared. "Man I'm tired of this thing! What the hell does it want?"

Ethan just looked back at Logan and said, "Your soul." As he just lay there looking up at the ceiling he was still wondering how to get rid of an unwanted ghost. As his eyes closed, Logan hoped the blood on the floor would simply vanish. Logan hopped out of bed and headed for the shower. "Hey man! don't be in there all day either. You know I have to get in there."

Logan popped his head out of the shower. "Yell, Yell! I hear you!" he chided

As the water started to run cold it also began to feel mushy. Logan looked up at the shower head and saw blood dripping. It came out slowly and started to form into Mr. Benjamin Jackson. Logan quickly jumped out of the shower and started yelling Until he fell over out of the tub and hit his head. Ethan came running into the bathroom. "What! What's wrong? ... What happened? Are you alright?"

Logan jumped to his feet and pointed. "Look! It's that thing again!" When Ethan pulled the shower curtain back, though, all he saw was clear running water. Ethan turned around and asked, "Are you sure that's what you saw?"

Logan turned, then looked back at Ethan. "Yes! I saw the old man again, only this time it was coming out of the shower head."

All Ethan could do was look at the water. "Okay! Okay!" as Ethan put his hand on Logan's shoulder, "Calm down, you're getting yourself all worked up." The more Logan would look at the shower head, the more he could imagine seeing Mr. Jackson standing there in their shower.

Logan snatched his shoulder away from Ethan. "I'm not crazy, I know what the hell I saw. He was standing right there." He turned and pointed as if he was still looking at the shower head. Mr. Jackson had indeed disappeared once more. Ethan looked back at Logan, "Well, it's my turn to get in the shower. Okay? You go ahead and get dressed I'll be out shortly."

As they arrived at school Ethan turned and looked at Logan. "Remember we can't tell a soul what happened this week. And try not to tell none of your friends either, Okay?"

Logan just turned his head away and started to stare out of the car window. "Yeah, sure, tell no one."

The Matthew brothers had begun to walk up to the school grounds when they noticed some of their friends were flagging them down. "Hey, there goes the Matthew brothers! We over here." One of their friends shouted out.

Ethan and Logan walked over to the picnic tables where most of their guy friends hang out. John turned and looked at the Matthew brothers. "Hey where you guys been? We've been looking all over for you." Logan turned and looked at Ethan again, then turned back at his friend John.

"We had a family issue but we are Okay for right now."

Ethan began to look all around the school yard just to make sure that the ghost of Mr. Benjamin Jackson was not following them. Ethan hurried up as he turned and punched Logan on the arm, while still looking at the fellas. "Hey, you guys let's go inside... we don't want to be late for class. You do know how Mrs. Johnson can get if you are late for her class." The boys started to laugh.

As they all began to walk into the building. Logan stopped in the middle of the hallway and started to notice the blood on the lockers. As he took a deep breath in with his eyes closed John came up behind him and put his hand on to Logan's shoulder. Logan jumped, "Man! What the hell!" Logan grabbed his chest holding on to it for dear life. "You scare the hell out of me!"

John turned around and looked at the other guys and started to laugh. "What?! What do you mean? I scare you. Not the 'Big Bad Logan'! I scare you. Wow!" John laughed even more as did the other boys. Logan turned and looked back at Ethan with a scared face. As if Mr. Jackson was standing right next to him. When

Logan turned and looked back at John he was met with, "Okay man!... why are you so jumpy? You're acting like you have just seen a ghost. Loosen up!" John lifted his hand and patted Logan on the back, and then the gentleman went their own separate ways. As the bell rang Logan looked back at Ethan and gave him a smirk, then both of the Matthew brother's went into their classroom.

"Good Morning class..." Ms. Cooper began as she walked in as if she was in a hurry. "Today I will be filling in for Mrs. Johnson. So please, the same respect that you give her – you should give to me." The class turned and looked at each other, then back at Ms. Cooper.

"Wow!" Logan hollered out. "I have never seen anyone with those type of legs before. She can teach me anytime." The whole class burst out with laughter.

Then Ms. Cooper stopped and turned around in the middle of the floor to stare back at the class. "Okay class, please! Settle down, I don't want to send anyone out on my first day here." Logan had begun to laugh a little harder, but when he looked up at Ms. Cooper his smile started to leave his face slowly.

As he saw the black shadow moving slowly from behind Ms. Cooper, then slowly move in front of the classroom Logan jumped up from his seat and hollered out "No!" The entire class looked up at Logan with serious silent looks. Ms. Cooper walked over towards Logan.

Then when she was able to look square at him and ask, "Are you alright my dear?" Logan was still in shock as he was still watching the black shadow move all around the room. Trying to get his attention, Ms. Cooper had called Logan's name three times. "Logan, Logan ... Logan dear! Are you alright?" As she snapped her fingers three times near his face Logan jumped and began to look at Ms. Cooper.

"Yeah, I'm Okay. I just need to get a drink of water." Logan went out the door as he began to walk down the hallway. He began to feel a cool breeze blowing up against his face. Logan stopped and turned around from front to back, to see if he could see the ghost's face appear.

Logan walked towards the water fountain and started drinking the cold water. Then as he lifted up his head he saw Mr. Benjamin Jackson standing right beside him. Logan fell to his knees. As the ghost began to whisper, "I want your soul, I want my revenge," Logan began to back up and he nearly tripped over his own two feet as he ran and slipped all over the hallway floor. Logan ran behind the lockers and started to duck down. This way the ghost couldn't see him. Logan thought to himself, 'If I sit here for a while, maybe it will leave,' but the ghost of Mr. Benjamin Jackson could hear him breathing. The black shadow moved in very slowly over the lockers. Logan felt the cool breeze once again. He looked up over his head to find the shadow standing directly over him. Logan tried to make a run for it. But the shadow was too quick as it grabbed him. The shadow of Mr. Jackson picked Logan up off of his feet and silently opened its mouth.

As it began to suck the breath out of Logan he began to turn blue and pale. The more he was tried to fight off the ghost, the more Mr. Jackson started to clearly appear. Logan looked at the face of Mr. Jackson now appearing with a half face, still half ghostly. All he could do was silently cry with tears running down his face.

As the bell rang Ethan came out of his classroom and he looked down, he noticed that Logan's diamond cuff bracelet was on the floor. Ethan bent down to pick up his brother's bracelet. As he started to go around the school hall and ask everyone nearby if they had seen his little brother, most classmates turned and looked at Ethan in a weird way. Every one just shook their head and walked away.

Ethan then heard a squealing noise, but he didn't know exactly where it was coming from. As the sound got louder the closer he reasoned he was getting. When he approached the lockers he saw Logan up in the air with feet dangling and his skin leaving his body. He quickly ran over to try and save his little brother.

Logan began yelling the ghost's name, "Mr. Benjamin Jackson!" but all the shadow did was turn around and open his mouth and say, "Now this is my revenge, I have both of you right where I want you." The shadow slowly twirled, coming down with Logan in his shadow hands.

The ghost lifted up his arm and tossed Logan over onto the lockers. The black and half human shadow began to rise up toward the ceiling and started to spread dust all over Logan and Ethan. "I want your soul. Your soul is now mine." The shadow kept repeating over and over as Ethan started to gag for air. He then fell face first on the floor. Ethan reached his hand into his pocket and took out the name tag of Mr. Jackson and pointed it directly at the black shadowy ghost. When Mr. Jackson looked down and saw his name tag in Ethan's hand. The black dusty shadow twirled and whirled all around in a circle, "No! You can't do this to me, I want my revenge, I want your soul!" Slowly the voice of Mr. Benjamin Jackson started to disappear.

# Chapter 7

Ethan started to crawl his way over by Logan. He grabbed and pulled on his brother, then held him and rocked back and forth. Suddenly he let out a loud cry. Everyone ran over to see what was going on. All they could do was look and stare. John had bent down to put his hand on Ethan's shoulder, but Ethan snatched his shoulder away. Ethan looked up at everyone and said, "Get away from me, leave us alone! Don't act like you care about my brother! You all hated him, so please leave me alone." As he was still holding on tight, Ms. Cooper walked over and bent down and touched his hair with a light stroke.

"Ethan, dear, let me help you please!"

All Ethan could do was hold his head down looking at his brother and cry. "Why! Why us, he kept on telling me that we need to tell someone. But I wouldn't let him. I wouldn't let him, Ms.

Cooper." Ethan held Logan close to his chest when all of a sudden Logan let out a big cough.

As he opened his eyes and stared at Ethan, the latter was still holding on tight with Logan burried in his chest. Logan yelled out, "I can't breathe dammit, Ethan! Get off of me, you are holding me too freaking tight. Let go!" Ethan looked down and began to laugh, all Ethan could do was hold his little brother in his arms with a smile upon his face.

"Man I thought you had left me for a moment, don't you ever scare me like that again, or I will kill you myself."

As the two Matthew brother's held one another tightly they swore to each other they would never leave each other's side. Logan looked up at Ethan, with tears in his eyes, "I'm so sorry for what I put you through big brother. Will you forgive me?"

All Ethan could do was smile as he got up off the floor. He looked down at Logan. "Forgive you huh! After all you put me thought and your little red butt wants me to forgive you."

Ms. Cooper turned and looked at both brothers, "Okay boys calm down. We have the whole school looking at us. So please: make up and go back to class and then we will discuss what just happened, Okay Boys?"

Ethan look at Ms. Cooper then looks back at Logan. "I think the both of you are crazy. Do you know what the hell this kid put me through the entire school year?"

Logan got off of the floor and looked at Ethan. "Wait! What? What's all that mess I miss you Logan, and don't leave me crap huh? What's all that for? Entertainment, a show, a circus, what was it Ethan? Tell me or you really want me out of your life?"

Ethan just looked down, and then back up at Logan.

"Yeah! It was all a show but I can't live without you no matter what we go through. You are still my little brother even though you are a big pain in the butt. I wouldn't trade you in for nothing."

Logan steps back and looks at Ethan and then looks around their classmates. "Stop! Stop with your shenanigans and being dishonest and your lies, Ethan."

Ethan looked at Logan and pulled him by his arm, "Get over here! Like I said, I would miss your butt and I wouldn't trade it in for nothing. No ghost, no money... well, I might trade you in for some money. For a couple of thousands, but yeah I don't think I would trade you." Logan stepped back and looked at Ethan when all of the sudden the lights started to blink off and on. Everyone had started to look around and wonder why or what was going on.

All of the students had started to get loud and moody, then Ms. Cooper took out her phone and operated the flashlight app so everyone would calm down. "Okay! Everyone lets not get all 'hay, wow!' Everyone needs to calm down at this moment. Now..." as Ms. Cooper shouted out from the top of her lungs. Everyone had stopped and began to look around. "Now that I have your attention..." as Ms. Cooper opened her mouth to say what she needed the students to do next instead she let out a scream. When the lights came back on there was no Ms. Cooper. Everyone was wondering where she had vanished to. However, Logan and Ethan turned and looked at one another as they knew right then and there where Ms. Cooper had gone to.

Logan had tried to take up the front of the group and speak, but as he did, he saw the thick red blood that had started to drip out onto his hands. He started to back up. Then he turned and looked up at Ethan, all Ethan could do was watch with his mouth open.

John hollered out about where all the blood was coming from, but everyone had started to move and even run for the door. Ethan had put his hands in the air. "Wait! Everyone I know you are scared but we have to stay together, or it is going to be a big mess.

So please listen to my brother and I so we can get you out of here safe."

John looked at both of the Matthew brothers and pointed. "You're the ones that got us in this crap and bring whatever that thing is up in here, and you got Ms. Cooper killed! Now you want all of us to die too! I'm getting the hell out of here!v You all can stay if you want to be killed!"

As John kept yelling on. Ethan and Logan had started to raise their voices, "Look as far as we know... well, we don't know what or who this thing is. So please let's stay together so we can help you. We promise we will get you to safety!"

John turned around and hollered out, "Safety huh? You can get all these people to safety? Yeah, right!

Ethan looked over at Logan and then back at John. "Naw, we're going to leave your little whining ass right here. Now, say another word!"

All John could do was fold his arms, and walk on the other side of the room.

After the Matthew brothers had gotten everyone to calm down, Ethan took out the name tag of Mr. Benjamin Jackson and showed it to Logan. "I think this is how we are going to get rid of the unwanted ghost."

Logan stepped back and looked wide-eyed at Ethan, "I just hope you know what you're doing. Because this damn thing is really getting on my last nerve. I can't sleep or eat because every time I close my eyes I see this ugly thing, and it's starting to make me sick in my ass."

Ethan just looked at Logan like he had lost his last mind. "Look! All we have to do is to make sure that we get this ghost to look at his name tag and hopefully then it will vanish."

"And if don't then what? What are we going to do next Mr. Ethan with the plan?"

Ethan had held his head back and started to squinch his eyes tightly together, as if he could shoot Logan with them. "Okay then, Mr. Logan, what's your plan then huh?!"

Logan had started to walk away then turned around and said, "Don't tell anybody!" With a big smile upon his face. All Logan could do was laugh and hold his stomach.

Ethan squinched his eyes a little more tight and then opened them up wide. "Oh! you thank this is funny right? Okay, well when the ghost has your little ass in the air again, don't you holler for me. For real Logan what are we going to do with these people? We can't just let them die."

Logan had stopped laughing and turned around and looked at his brother. "What do you mean 'we can't let them die'? Hell didn't they let me die, so why can't I pay the price back, and let them die? It's a win-win situation, right, bro?"

"No, bro," As Ethan looked disappointedly at him, "that's not right they didn't have anything to do with what happened to this old man that you killed. Now you have gone too far with this Logan. Maybe I should have just let the ghost just kill you when he had a chance."

All Logan could do was look up at Ethan and say, "Well, I am already dead. Thanks big brother for everything you have ever done for me."

Ethan had tears in his eyes when he apologized, "I didn't mean it that way, I'm sorry. Please we really need to work together on this thing. Logan. Logan!" as he kept on calling his name the more Logan would stand there with a big happy smile on his face. Ethan had walked a little closer to Logan and just started to stare at the way he was smiling and holding his head. Eventually he had to ask, "Are you Okay man? You look kind of different. And why you are holding your head sideways and foam from the mouth? What the hell is wrong with you man?" As Ethan got a little closer to Logan the ghost of Mr.Benjamin Jackson had started to appear on Logan's face; Half-human and half-ghost.

"Like I said before; I want my revenge. I want your soul." Logan's head kept turning side-to-side. All Ethan could think to do was back away and put his hand in his pocket to take out the name tag of Mr. Benjamin Jackson. The half human and half ghost of Logan looked down at Ethan's hand and asked, "What you got there my big brother?" Ethan took his hand out and held it up in the air so the ghost could see the silver name tag. Logan began to back up and look wild-eyed. "No! You will not kill me this time, I have what you want. So, Big brother Ethan... Why don't you come and join me?" As the ghost and Logan drew closer Ethan had to back away while still holding his hand in the air. Logan looked at Ethan and asked, "What's wrong... it doesn't work?" As the ghost let out a big laugh Ethan threw it into the Logan's mouth. Logan grabbed at his throat and started to gag for air.

Ethan yelled, "Out! Let my little brother go you ugly thing!" However, the more he demanded, "Let my little brother go," the more the ghost of Mr. Jackson had started to come over Logan's body.

Ethan looked up at the ghost of Mr.Benjamin Jackson and started to cry. "I love you man, Logan, this is no lie this time. I really do love you. Please don't leave me. You said we would never leave one another's side, no matter how tough things get." Logan, do you hear me? I know you're there, please don't leave me, bro I love you." The ghost had started to twirl around and around in circles. Then black dust in the air had started to smoke up the school hallway. Ethan thought to himself, 'If I keep saying I love you the ghost would let him go.' As Ethan kept on saying he loves Logan, the more thick black ghost came out of Logan. The black and white smoke got thick and heavy. Ethan had dropped to his knees and began to pray. "Lord I'm coming to with an open heart. All I ask upon you is to please protect him, and help me bring back my little brother. I promise I will keep him safe, amen."

As the ghost twirled his way out of Logan suddenly the image of Mr. Benjamin Jackson looked down at the Matthew brothers and said, "This is not over, I will be back." Logan had dropped to the floor as soon as Mr. Jackson came out of his body.

Logan's soul was so weak and thin that he couldn't hardly stand up. Ethan ran over to Logan, "Hey man! I got you, yes, I got you. Everything is going to be Okay."

# Chapter 8

Ethan looked Logan over and said, as much to himself, "Not again! I hope you are not trying to leave me, not after all we have been through. We have so much more we have to do like finish school together." C'mon, please Logan! Don't leave me. What would I do without you?"

Logan turned his head to face Ethan, "There you go again with that crap. Just get the hell out of my face and let me get up. I know when I get myself together I'm gonna kill that ghost."

Ethan leaned over sideways to face him, "You can't kill something that's already dead, Logan. You do know that right? Mr. I-know-everything." Logan just look at him up and down and started to laugh again. Ethan stepping back, asked, "What's your problem, and why are you so damn happy? You almost died here twice today. Are you sure you're Okay?"

Logan took a deep breath in and then let out a cold wind of air out of his mouth. "Yes, I'm alright. Never felt better. Like you said we have to get these people to safety." Ethan just looked at him with a weird expression and then walked away. The more Ethan would look at Logan, the more his face appeared like that of Mr. Jackson.

Ethan shook his head and put his hand on his forehead. "Now! I know I just didn't see what I thought I saw. Naw! That can't be... yeah I'm seeing things. there is no way that this ghost has gotten into my little brother," he said to himself. "Get it together Ethan. It's no time for you to be tripping over something that you might or thought you saw. However, we have to get these people to safety quick and fast." As he started to gather up everyone, Ethan had looked over at Logan and called his name, "Hey Logan man!"

Logan turned around with the look of the dead man's face upon him again. "What the hell you want, and why are you calling me like you lost your damn mind?"

Ethan stopped and dropped his mouth open with a look of disbelief that Logan was talking to him that way. "Wait! What? What do you mean, why am I calling you? To help me get these people to safety you jerk! And what the ... nevermind, I just do it myself." Meanwhile Ethan was trying to get all of the students to safety and out of the building.

Logan was transforming again into Mr. Benjamin Jackson, but the soul of Logan was trying very hard to fight it off.

John came running towards the Matthew brothers yelling, "We still need to find Ms. Cooper! We have to help her get out of here, too! It wouldn't be fair if we escape and she is still stuck here in this raggedy old building!" John stopped and then turned around to see everyone around him. "So are we going to find her or what, or we are just going to let her die? We can't just let her die like that!"

*Linda Spence Howard*

Logan walked over behind John and put his hand on John's shoulder and began to laugh. "Well, I guess she would have to vanish like the rest of them, Right?"

John jumped back and looked at Logan's face. "What the hell is wrong with your face man?" The more John backed up the more Logan's face changed.

Logan looked at John and began to smile, "What do you mean my friend? I am perfectly fine never felt better."

Ethan ran over and got between the both of them. "Okay! Well that's enough, you two. Now, it's time for you both to help me get these people to safety." As he turned and looked over at John, "Yes, John we will find Ms. Cooper, but right now my concern is these students and their safety. So can you help me with that?

John turned and looked at Ethan, "Yeah, I can... but keep your creepy little brother away from me."

Ethan just looked at John. In his soft voice "Hell, I wish I could keep him away from me, also. But I can't because he is my little brother. And furthermore, I promised him that I will be there no matter what. Even if he does look like that old man."

John stopped with a puzzled look upon his face. "Wait! What old man?"

Ethan looked at John and then waved him off. "Nevermind... look, we have to get these people to another location so come on."

John looked at Ethan and then back at Logan. 'Yeah it's something fishy about these two. They been acting kind of weird sent they got here this morning, and I'm going to find out what them two have gotten into, but how? I know, I'll just snoop around and then follow them and see what they've been up to. Yeah, that's what I'll do. We'll see what is so secretive about the Matthew brothers.

Later on that afternoon the Matthew brothers had finally gotten everyone to safety including themselves. As they got home they noticed that Mr. Haywood was on their front door step waiting. Ethan walked up on the porch looking strangely at the visitor. "Hey there, Mr. Haywood, what are doing over so late in the afternoon?" with a smile on his face as if he was shocked that he was there.

"I can't find my twin brother."

The Matthew boys just looked at him for a moment then came back with, "We didn't know you had a twin brother Mr. Haywood."

He turned and looked at both brothers. "Yeah, his name is Benjamin Jackson, and I'm Haywood Jackson. The Matthew brothers looked at each other. Mr. Haywood turned and looked back at the boys. "I put in a missing report for him. I can't imagine you boys separated from one another. Me and my twin are inseparable. We do everything together."

Ethan stared at Mr. Haywood and then back at Logan. "Yeah, you are right Mr. Haywood, I couldn't imagine myself without my little Logan." With a smirk on his face while looking at Logan. Ethan began to pull Logan into the house. "Well if we hear anything, we will let you know.

Mr. Haywood Jackson turned around as he was about to step off the porch, "Please do, because I really do need my twin brother."

As the Matthew brothers got into the house, Logan turned to Ethan, "Now what are we going to do? The ghost that keeps hunting us is Mr. Haywood's twin brother, and we both done kill him."

Ethan pointed his finger at Logan, "Don't start nothing you can't finish... and stop blaming me for something you have done. You created this monster so now you have to fix it. I'm done with you and this damn ghost." Ethan turned and walked away.

Logan came running behind him, "oh no, we in this mess together big brother. If you like it or not you are a part of this crime, too, so I suggest you own up to it." Logan's face had started to change once more.

Ethan's eyes opened up big. "Uh, Logan?!" As Ethan started backing back from Logan, "What's wrong with your face? That's twice today your face looked like that old man. Are you Okay, man?"

Logan shook his head while holding onto it. As he rubbed his hand down his face. Then he looks back up at Ethan. With a slight grin and his eyes turning bloodshot red Logan looked up and smiled. "Yes, I'm good, just don't patronize me. I have a lot going on in my head right now so, whatever you say or do, own up to it or else there will be a problem."

Ethan turned on Logan, "Are you threatening me?"

Logan stopped and turned, "No that was a promise. Like I said, own up to what you did." As Logan walked towards Ethan he bumped him with his shoulder blade.

Ethan threw his hands up in the air. He went behind Logan into the Living room, "Look, I get it, you don't want to take the blame all by yourself."

Logan stopped and turned around and just looked at Ethan.

All of sudden a cold wind of air came blowing all around the living room, and Ethan and Logan looked at one another. Then Ethan had put his arm over his face as the black dust swirled all around the brothers. Logan bent over and grabbed his stomach. He crawled towards the front door. The more the pain would hit Logan's stomach, causing him to double over, the more of Mr. Benjamin Jackson would twirl his way out of Logan's mouth. Logan's face had turned pale green and started to look like a dead man. All Ethan could do was push himself into a corner and ball up into a knot.

# Chapter 9

The black dusty shadow of Mr. Benjamin Jackson had finally came out of Logan. Twirling itself all around the room. "You thought you could get away from me, didn't you? I came to get what's mine, and I'm going to get it! Your souls will be all mine!" The ghost let out a loud cry of laughter at the Matthew brothers. The ghost of Mr. Jackson kept twirling around and around and repeating, "I want my revenge! I want your soul!"

When a knock came upon the front door the black dusty, foggy ghost of Mr. Jackson started to disappear back into Logan. Ethan jumped up and ran to the door, and immediately flung it open. Standing there was Mr. Haywood with his shiny bald head and his back turned towards the front door. Ethan hollered out "Oh my God! Thank goodness it's you!"

Linda Spence Howard

Mr. Haywood turned around and said. "Why would you say that son? What's wrong? You acting like something scares the daylights out of you boys." As Mr. Haywood started to walk into the house, he noticed how cold it was in there. He looked around and asked, "Where are your parents, and why is it so cold in here?"

Ethan looked at Logan and then back at Mr. Haywood, "Well they hum... well I mean, they are out of town. Yeah they are out of town to go see their mother... I mean my grandmother. Yeah that's where they went." At this Ethan grinned. "He looked back at Mr. Haywood once more. "So again, tell us why are you here.

Mr. Haywood looked puzzled for a moment. "Ah yeah I came to tell you that the police is working on finding my twin brother." Both of the Matthew brothers stared at one another until all of sudden Logan bent over and grabbed his stomach.

Mr. Haywood looked at Logan curiously. "What's wrong you, my boy are you Okay?" Logan's face had started to turn pale green as a dead man's face again, but before he could lift his head up Ethan jumped right in front of Logan and pushed Mr. Haywood out the front door. "Wait... Wait, your brother need's help. I think we should call someone, or call your parents." Ethan was still trying to push Mr. Haywood out the door. "We will be Okay. Thanks for everything!"

As Ethan slammed the front door behind Mr. Haywood. Mr. Jackson twirled his way back out of Logan once again.

Ethan looked up at the ghost and said, "What do you want from us? Why do you keep following us? Please leave us alone! We don't have what you want."

The thick black shadow started to cover the front room once again. Mr. Jackson simply laughed, "You think that you don't have what I want? Just look down at yourselves and think about what I need and want."

The ghost twirled around and around, but then all of a sudden stopped. The dusty black shadow started to clear up.

Ethan, used the break to turn and look Logan over. "Are you alright?"

Logan rolled over on his back and stared up at the ceiling as he asked, "Do you think that we need to tell Mr. Haywood about what we did to his twin brother?

Ethan took a deep breath in and twirled his tongue around in his mouth. "Okay, I'm going to ask you this: is that Logan talking or is that damn ghost again. Because if you think for one second, that I'm going to tell someone about this delusional crazy ghost then you and that ghost have lost y'all's damn minds? What the hell is wrong with you? Am I going to tell someone? You really have lost it haven't you?"

All Logan could do was look at him and turn on his side. "I'm just getting tired of this ghost taking over my body. You have seen what it could do to me when it takes control. I have no control of my body when it's in me. Please Ethan we have to tell someone, we have to stop this thing."

Ethan slid down to the floor, leaning against the front door, and sat on along with Logan. "So, if we're going to tell someone about this ghost, I mean Mr. Jackson, we could go to jail for the rest of our lives. Logan, do you want that?" Logan closed his eyes. "Hey man, do you hear me talking to you or is that Mr. Jackson?"

Logan opened up his eyes and looked at Ethan, "No stupid it's me and, yes, I hear you loud and clear... Jackass."

"All I'm saying is that this thing is really getting on my nerves, and if we don't stop this thing it's going to kill both of us." The expectation in the room became palpable so Logan continued, "Well, are you going to tell someone or not, Ethan?" By the time Ethan went to say something Mr. Benjamin Jackson had started to return back into Logan, who curled up into a knot holding his

*Linda Spence Howard*

stomach and rocking back and forth. "Oh my god this pain is really unbearable, Ethan make it stop please!"

Ethan's look at Logan turned into a stare as he crawled his way over by the front window. Logan was steady turn pale green as Mr. Jackson started to form. Ethan tried to get up off the floor to try to make a run for it, but it was too late, Logan's body had already transformed back into Mr. Jackson's, and Ethan was trapped against the wall looking at Logan's body as it took on the form of the old man at the cemetery. The vision was complete in it's shaggy hair, blue overall jumper, and black baseball cap.

Mr. Jackson got up off the floor and walked over to Ethan with his head turning from one side to the other. "Well! Well! Well! I must say we do meet again." Ethan went to make a run for it again, but Mr. Jackson stuck his hand out and grabbed Ethan by the throat. The ghost held him up in the air with one hand, and then tossed him up against the wall. "Please Ethan my boy, don't play with me! Just give me what I want and we will be just fine."

Mr. Jackson slowly walked over to Ethan again and tried to reach for him, but as he reached out his hand for Ethan's neck another tap came at the front door. Mr. Jackson turned and looked at the door. Ethan yelled out, "Help! Help me! This thing is trying to kill me."

Mr. Jackson took his hand and put it over Ethan's mouth. "You better not say another word! If you do, I'm going to suck the life right out of you. Do you understand me, my boy?

With tears coming down his face and with his mouth covered harshly Ethan found all that he could do was nod his head. Mr. Jackson started to turn back into Logan. Ethan's eyes opened wide with more tears still flowing down his face. It took a moment, but Logan opened up the front door and there was Mr. Haywood standing there yet again.

"Yes, may I help you?"

Mr. Haywood turned around and stared at Logan up and then down. "Are you Okay, my son?" Mr. Haywood immediately tried to walk into the house.

Logan pushed Mr. Haywood back a step, "Yes I'm fine, what do you want? Is it something I can help you with?"

Mr. Haywood, taken aback, glared at Logan, "Well, yes there is. I need to see your brother about the newspaper he borrowed from me yesterday.

Logan squinted at Mr. Haywood, paused and then said, "We didn't see you yesterday and we are kinda of busy right now. So can you come back another time? Like years from now."

Mr. Haywood frowned and looked back at Logan. "Come back years from now? No, I need my paper, and I want it now." Logan's facial expression had started to change again into Mr. Benjamin Jackson, "I told you that there is no paper here. Now get lost kid, you're bothering me."

Mr. Haywood looked at Logan with a puzzled look. "Hey my twin brother used to call me that. Did you know him?"

Logan was getting mad and madder. "No! I don't and I don't want to, old man. Now please, go away!"

Yet Mr. Haywood was still trying to make his way into the house.

All of a sudden Ethan yelled out, "Help me, Mr. Haywood!" With that Mr. Haywood pushed his way into the house and saw Ethan lying on the floor. When Mr. Haywood turned around to look at Logan again all he saw was his twin brother standing in front of him.

"What the hell!" As Mr. Haywood's eyes opened wide, he could not believe what he had just seen.

# Chapter 10

Mr. Haywood fell back a step to get a good look at what he thought was his twin brother. No that can't be... could it? Mr. Haywood knew he must be still looking at Logan, but with Benjamin's face on him! He stared with his mouth wide open. "Benjamin is that you... I mean, where have you been? I have been looking all over for you!" Yet all Benjamin Jackson did was look at Mr. Haywood. "Say something damnit! Where have you been B.J.? Why haven't you called me? Answer me for crying out loud." Ethan got up off the floor.

"That's not your brother that's the ghost of your brother and he has taken over my little brother's body."

Mr. Haywood turned and looked at Ethan, then back at Logan. "Wait... What? What you mean that... this is the ghost of my brother. What the hell have you boys done with my brother Benjamin!"

As Ethan had made a move towards Mr. Haywood, the ghost of Mr. Jackson started to come alive. Also seemingly, the more deeply the ghost was in Logan's body the more Mr. Jackson had started to show. Ethan then had to step back, "I will explain later, but right now, we have to get the hell out of here. The fog had covered the living room so heavily Mr. Haywood and Ethan could hardly see a thing.

"What the hell is going on?"

Ethan yelled across the room, "Well, you just bring your old tail so we can get the hell out of here before he takes your damn soul, or whatever else he came for. Look I will explain to you on the way out of here. Right now, we have no time!"

Benjamin Jackson had started out with a loud cry. "I want your soul, I want my revenge!"

Ethan grabbed Mr. Haywood by the hand, "Now, see? Can we get the hell out of here before I become a dead kid?"

Ethan and Mr. Haywood had started fumbling their way through the house when all of sudden the fog began to clear. Ethan turned and looked for Mr. Haywood, but in the split second he turned around Mr. Haywood was gone. Ethan went to call for him, "Mr. Haywood, dammit?! This old man is starting to get on my last nerves.... Hey! If he took your soul that fine with me, but if he didn't, bring your old saggy butt out. Man, this is why I don't have company. Mr. Haywood!" The more he called his name the more it seemed silent. Ethan checked each room to see if Mr. Haywood had ducked into one of them, however, every room he checked there was no Mr. Haywood. As he went up stairs to check the bedroom.

Ethan heard the ghost of Mr. Benjamin Jackson again, "I want your soul. I want my revenge!"

Ethan had stopped at the top of the stairs and started to look around. He walked a little slower as he thought to himself... 'Damn, I forgot the name tag.' But it was a little too late, Ethan was already in one of the bedrooms looking for something to kill the unwanted ghost.

'What can I find in here to try to stop him,' thought Ethan as he peeked around the corner into the bedroom. He noticed that the door was cracked halfway open. 'Wait! I know I didn't crack that door.' The moment Ethan went toward the door to open it, the door slammed shut. 'Damn! now I know that ghost is here with me.' So he yelled out "Okay, Logan or Mr. Jackson, whichever one you are look, I'm not playing any more games and, no, you can't have my damn soul!" The more Ethan talked the more the door swung back open. "Oh, I see, you want to keep playing games. Okay, that's why I have your twin brother, and you can't have him. Now what, Mr. Benjamin or Logan, I think..." Ethan's hands had started to tremble as he walked towards the door. He took a deep breath before he reached for the door handle. As soon as he pushed open up the door there he saw Mr. Haywood standing. "What the hell? Where have you been? I have been looking all over this house for you, Mr. Haywood."

Mr. Haywood looked at him as he held on to his chest. "I hid in the utility room, then the fog had started to get thick so I ran. Now, can you tell me what is going on with you and your brother, and how my brother Benjamin got to do with all of this mess?" All Ethan could do was look at Mr. Haywood and walk away. "Hey don't you walk away from me, you still have to tell me what the hell is going on and what you did..."

"Okay!" Ethan hollered out, "My brother and I were at a cemetery one night, and we had started to play around... and this old man was there, I think he was working or something, I'm not sure. Anyway, the old man said something and Logan hit him over the head with an iron pipe. So now this damn ghost done back for his revenge. I think he was your brother, Mr. Benjamin Jackson, Please Mr. Haywood don't be mad at me. This ghost or thing has my little brother and I need your help."

Haywood Jackson had stepped back and looked at Ethan. "Why should I help you and your brother when you killed mine? Do you think for one second I should kill you or better yet turn you tail end in to the police? What you thank Ethan?"        The more Mr. Haywood and Ethan went back and forth at one another the less they noticed Logan walking up and then standing in the doorway. "May I ask you two what the hell you are fighting about and why you two are not helping me kill this damn ghost that keeps on attacking me."

Ethan looked up at Logan, "Logan is that really you or is that Mr. Jackson?"

Logan walks into the room and pushes Ethan on the floor and kicks him. "Naw, Butt wipe, could Mr. Jackson do that?"

Ethan jumped off the floor and gripped Logan and started to kiss him on his forehead. Logan pushed Ethan back. "Man, don't try none of that funny stuff. I don't get down like that and, furthermore, we have no time to stand here being lovey-dovey."

Ethan studied Logan, "Are you sure that this is you and not that ghost of Mr. Jackson?"

Logan cocked his head and looks right at Ethan. Do you want me to push you down again? Just say it and I'll do it."

"No there is no need for that I'm just so happy to see bro."

When the Matthew brothers went to hug each other one more time Logan looked around. "Hey... where did Mr. Haywood go?" Ethan tilted his head back and looked around at Logan's observation. "Wait! He was just here a moment ago. Now where did he go? Now we have to look for him again." Ethan turned back to Logan.

"The hell if we do. Do you know how long it took me to find that old man? I'm not going to search for him again. Hell no"!"

Logan turned and said, "He is our neighbor, and plus we did kill his brother."

Ethan abruptly started pacing back and forth then he stopped and looked at Logan. "There you go again with that mess: 'We killed the old man'! I already told you that I'm not going down for something you did. So quit saying we 'cause *we* have done nothing to this old man."

Logan stepped back and looked down, "Yeah, yeah... I already know: You are not going down, you keep right on saying the same thing over and over again. But you keep forgetting we did this crime together big bro. So, if you like or not you are the blame just as well as I am. So come on and let's find old man Haywood and then put you in the shower because you stink."

Ethan ran back down stairs to try to find the name tag that had been left on the coffee table, but when he looked it was gone. Ethan turned and looked at Logan when he arrived in the room, "Did you take the name tag off the coffee table?"

Logan frowned and poke his lips out like a duck. "Really" How you suppose am I going to move a name tag when the damn ghost of Benjamin Jackson has my soul" Ethan, I think you need to take a cold shower because you are hallucinating. And what do you need the name tag for anyhow?"

Ethan pointed at Logan, "To make sure that Mr. Jackson is not in you."

Logan broke it down for Ethan, "Oh hell, he is still in me, but just try not to say something that's going to piss him off. Okay?"

"Yeah sure, so this ghost is still in you? how are we supposed to get it out of you?"

Logan made a face at him. "You are starting to piss off this thing in me. My stomach is flipping over here, so if I were you... I would just shut the hell up, and go find Mr. Haywood."

Both of Matthew brothers went looking for Mr. Haywood when a loud sound of thunder startled them. Ethan and Logan stopped and looked at one another. "Was that Mr. Jackson or was that your stomach?"

Logan looked at Ethan and said, "I think that was thunder, butt wipe. Would you cut it out playing and let's find this old man so we can get the hell out of here?"

Ethan stopped and looked at Logan, "You are forgetting that we do live here, right?"

Logan turned and looked at Ethan up and down with a strange look as if he didn't know that they live together. "Why the hell would you say something like that? Yes, I know we live here. What you think I'm crazy or something? Ethan went to open his mouth, then Logan turned around and said, "You better not let it out. Say it if you want to, and I will bring Mr. Benjamin out... Go ahead and say, I dare you." All Ethan could do was shake his head and walk away.

# Chapter 11

The more they were looking for Mr. Haywood, the more Logan's body was trying to change back into Mr. Benjamin Jackson. However, Logan was trying to fight off the ghost that was inside of him. Logan finally got to a point where he had to stop, turned and look at Ethan and say to him, "You must find Mr. Haywood by yourself. I can no longer walk along with you. This ghost that's in me, it's starting to get more and more stronger."

Ethan turned back to Logan, "I will not leave you alone with that ghost inside. We are in this together remember so please, Logan, fight it off." Ethan thought back and said to himself, 'did I just say that? I know I just didn't say that!' Then, "Look we have to keep moving or else we will never find Mr. Haywood."

Logan turned and looked at Ethan wearily and nodded his head. "Where do you think he could be in this big house?" Then Logan bent over to hold his stomach while still looking up at Ethan.

"I don't know!... but he has to be around here somewhere. Let's check the utility room – he was in there when the lights went out." The Matthew brothers had started to walk towards the utility room when all of sudden a strange sound occurred. Ethan stopped and turned as he looked back at Logan. "Did you hear that?" As he went to walk towards Logan the sound got louder. Ethan brough up Logan's eyes and asked, "Is that... that thing trying to come out of you? Because if it is he has to wait right about now"

Logan looked up at Ethan and said, "Very funny... Jackass! Let's keep moving. I'm starting to feel kinda weak here."


Ethan started to yell out, "Hey Mr. Haywood, can you hear me?" but the more he would call that name the more that Ethan could hear Logan. Ethan turned and looked Logan over and asked, "Are you Okay, bro? Do you need to sit down?" All Logan would do was hold on tight to his stomach.

"Yeah I'm Okay, just trying to keep this thing in me so it won't kill no one." Logan reached his hand out to Ethan, "Please I need you to go ahead without me."

Ethan stopped and turned back and looked at Logan, "No! I will not leave you here alone." Ethan had taken his hand while wondering, 'Damn, why do I keep saying that? What the hell is wrong with me?'

Logan looked up at Ethan With a pale dead man's face. "Okay man, what the hell is wrong with your face and why are you looking so pale?" Logan just lifted up his head with a big smile on it. Ethan stepped back. "Okay, Okay... at the time that I needed you the most, you go and bring out this damned thing again... Logan!" Ethan turned to make a run for it. Mr. Jackson started to creep out of Logan and tried to run Ethan down, but Ethan ran toward the basement. There he found Mr. Haywood laying on the floor.

Ethan went to nudge Mr. Haywood, but the old man was knocked out cold. Ethan had started to look around for something to wake Mr. Haywood up with. 'Well, I wonder if this smell from this nasty t-shirt will wake him.'

Mr. Haywood shook his head and opened his eyes. He saw Ethan standing over top of him. "Where am I?" Mr. Haywood turned and looked up Ethan.

Ethan bent down to help Mr. Haywood off the floor. "Look we have to get out of here, that thing done got back into my brother again, and I'm going to need your help. Please help me get my brother back Mr. Haywood!"

Mr. Haywood began to stand to his feet and look at Ethan with a look as if he wanted to kill Ethan himself. "I shouldn't help you, or your brother... after all; you did kill my twin brother."

Ethan cut Mr. Haywood off, "Look, I know you mad as hell with me and my brother for what we have done to your brother. But we do not have time to go back and forth with one another and debate on who is right and who is wrong. So, are you going to help me or not?" As they both shook hands the basement door started to shake and rattle. Ethan turned and looked at Mr. Haywood as he put one finger over his mouth, whispering, "Don't say anything..." They both started to look around to see if Mr. Jackson was in sight.

Mr. Haywood then started to cough, and he hurriedly put his hand over his mouth. Ethan turned and looked at him and said, "Shhh, you don't want that thing to get us now do you?" Mr. Haywood shook his head back and forth. "Come on, I think it's gone now. Let's see if we can get out of here and go find some help."

Mr. Haywood and Ethan walked towards the basement door. When Ethan opened it all he saw was Mr. Jackson standing there in his black overall jean pants. "I want my revenge... I want your soul!" Ethan quickly shut the basement door.

Ethan turned and looked at Mr. Haywood, "We are never going to get out of here.

Mr. Haywood looked all around the basement room. "What if we climb through that window without making any noise?"

Ethan looked over at the window and turned back to look at Mr. Haywood. "That Window!? I know damn well you are not talking about that window."

Mr. Haywood looked back at the window, again, "Yes! I'm talking about that window, and you need to watch your mouth young man, or I'm..."

Ethan stopped him and glared at Mr. Haywood. "Or you're going to what? What you're going to do is climb your old tail through that window, and go and find some help, so we can get the hell out of here?"

Indeed Mr. Haywood decided to climb through the window himself. Ethan looked nervously back and forth between the door then and Mr. Haywood's progress at climbing out. "Will you hurry up? You are starting to move like an old snail, for God's sake! By the time you get out this window that thing will be in here to kill the both of us." Mr. Haywood slid his way out of the window. Ethan ran behind several big brown brown boxes hoping that the ghost of Mr. Jackson wouldn't see him as the door swung open. A cool breeze came rushing in, and the big, black, dusty shadow had started to cover the entire basement. Ethan's eyes had started to water and he could not see a single thing. As he felt his way around without making any sound all he could feel was the cold heavy wind that was hitting up against his face. Ethan thought to himself,

'What if I held my breath in, so that way this thing will not know I'm here.' So Ethan decided to hold his breath for at least two minutes.

He let out his breath as softly as he could. But when he let it out... still all he saw was this thick black shadow smoke. Ethan covered his mouth as quickly as he could. 'No,' He thought to himself, 'this can't be! This thing can not be in me! I'm not ready to die yet!' Ethan stared at his hands as they started to shake. 'If only I could get back in the living room to get that name tag, I could kill this thing and save myself and my brother. Yeah! That's what I'll do.' Yet, the more he thought about the name tag of Mr. Jackson the more he got scared... and the more the black shadow covered of the basement. Ethan thought to himself once again, 'What if I could call out to my brother and see if it's really him or the ghost of Mr. Jackson.'

Ethan stood up slowly from behind the big boxes and started to call out his brother's name. "Logan! Can you hear me? It's me, your brother, Ethan." Everything fell silent, and Ethan got really scared. 'Man I wish Mr. Haywood was with me right about now. Where the heck did he go? Where did he go and find help at? In another state. Damn! He's taking a long time to get back here.' So he tried once more to call out Logan's name.

No answer, but when he closed his eyes for just a second, by the time Ethan opened them Logan was standing right in front of him. Ethan jumped back and knocked all of the boxes down. "Damn Logan! You scared the hell out of me. Why didn't you answer me when I just called you."

Logan made a face, "When did you call me? I just got down here. Here take this, because we're going to be needing it."

Ethan opened up his hand and looked down at it. There was the name tag of Mr. Benjamin Jackson looking new as if the name tag had never been touched. Ethan looked at Logan, "Wait...

how did you escape from the ghost?  And, how did you get his name tag?"

Logan turned around and said, "I fought him off with the name tag that was left on the coffee table.  I grabbed the name tag and put it up against my chest.  That's when it shot out of me and I fell to my knees." Ethan got up off the floor and slowly walked toward Logan.

"How do I know if it's really you?" Ethan stared at Logan, who just started back.  "Okay well, I'm going to ask you a couple of questions.  How old are you?"

Logan turned and looked at Ethan with a frown on his face.  "What? What kind of damn question is that?"  Ethan looked at him and then leaned his head back in exasperation.  "Well how old are you?  And what is my favorite color?"

"Okay, that's it... now it's time for me to ring your neck."

Ethan had ran to the other side of the basement.  "Man, I have to make sure that it's you."

Logan looked at him as if he wanted to take his head off.  "You ask me a stupid question like that again, and I will nail you to mom's Christmas tree.  Stop playing with me, Ethan!  And where the hell did Mr. Haywood get to?  I thought you two were together.  What happened Ethan?  Did the ghost get him, too?"

"No!  I sent him to get help."

Logan dropped his head and started to laugh.  "You damn idiot!  Why would you send an old man, not just an old man, but an old man whose brother we just killed?  Are you thinking Ethan?  Oh my God!  You couldn't been thinking.  What the Hell?"

"Look, he said he would go and find some help and come right back." Ethan went to the window and pointed.  "This is how he got out."

Logan looked over at the window, and his eyes got bigger

than fifty-cent-pieces. "Wait... you're telling me that you let an old man climb his way through a small-ass, baby window..."

Logan laughed and walked towards the basement door. "I'm going to my room and get some rest so we can figure out how to get rid of this ghost that's tearing up my life." He looked Ethan up and down, "I think you should get some rest, too. We have a big day tomorrow at school. We still have to find a way to get Ms. Cooper back without anyone noticing she was gone. Oh yeah, and try to keep up with that name tag, 'cause we damn sure going to need it."

# Chapter 12

Early the next morning both Matthew brothers got up for school and got dressed. Logan turned to Ethan as he finished putting on his shoes and said, "This has been one crazy week for us. I just hope when we get to school, that no one will ever remember what happened last week."

Ethan shot back at Logan, "You think not? We still haven't found Ms. Cooper yet, or found out why it's taken Mr. Haywood so long to find help."

Logan laughed again, "Oh, he went to find help alright, right to the police station."

Ethan studied Logan. "Do you think he would do that? I told him it was an accident."

Logan turned his head and looked at Ethan under eyes. "Sometimes I wonder about you. I just wonder wish one is the brightest. Oh wait, that's me."

Ethan looked at Logan as if he wanted to shoot him. "Logan, you know what you can do, right? Go to hell! And quit playing around."

"Look, we have to get ready for school."

As they pulled up to the school ground, they noticed how everyone was looking at them. Ethan leaned in and asked Logan in hushed tones, "Do you think they noticed about the ghost from last week."

After he leaned over and whispered to Logan the latter looked around and yelled out, "Naw, They didn't notice!" He jumped out of the driver's seat, then walked over where everyone was standing. "What's up John, did you miss me?" Logan asked with a big grin on his face. John looked at him with a strange look. "Well, hell, did anyone miss me?"

Ethan walked over to where Logan was. "Come on, I think we need to go Logan. They know what happened last week."

So as the Matthew brothers decided to walk away John yelled out, "Hey man! We miss you. We all miss you. As a matter of fact we were wondering if you know what happened to Ms. Cooper. She went missing last week around the time all of that commotion went on in the hallway." Logan stopped and turned around and stared.

"What do you mean Ms. Cooper is missing? Well, where the hell is she?"

John looked over at Ethan and then back to Logan. "I think that thing got her."

Logan's face had started to frown, "What thing? Yeah, you and my brother are losing it. And what do you mean 'that thing' got her? Ethan went to open his mouth, but Logan looked at him and said, "If you even think about what I think you are about to say; Don't! Because I do not want to hear it. Come on here. I'm going to be late for class messing around with you two clowns." Everyone entered into the building.

Logan then noticed how cold it had started to get. "Hey man, are you starting to get cold?"

Ethan turned and looked at Logan as if he knew that Mr. Jackson was about to appear. "No, but are you Okay?" As he stepped in front of Logan to look at him, with his head turned sideways, "Are you sure, Logan, that you're Okay?"

Logan backed away from Ethan, "Yeah, I'm Okay, and back the hell up off of me! Get out of my face you starting to creep me out."

All Ethan could do was to look at Logan as he walked away. John stoped and pulled Ethan by the arm. "Hey man, what's up with your brother? He's not seeing that thing again is he?"

Ethan turned on John as he pulled his arm away. "No, he's not and stop calling it 'that thing.' You are starting to freak me out."

John leaned his head back and then looked at the Matthew brothers as they walked away.

Ethan ran behind Logan trying to catch up to his head start. "Hey, man slow down. Damn, I'm trying to make sure you're Okay, Butt wipe!"

Logan stopped and took in a deep breath, "Yeah, I'm Okay, I just wish this thing would leave me alone. And you too. Well, let's get to class before we are too late."

Ethan stopped at the door and shot back at Logan, "Hey! Logan, man... I love you."

Logan stopped and frowned his face as he leaned his head back... "Man! I done told you: I don't do that funny stuff."

Ethan smiled. "Yeah you told me. See you after class."

Logan nodded his head, "Yeah, see you after class." Logan ran back to the door. "Wait, Ethan!"

Ethan stopped and turned around, "Yeah what is it?"

"What if you see Mr. Jackson and you can't get out of the classroom?"

Ethan just looked at Logan with a big smile on his face. "Hey man, don't worry, I'm going to be fine. And, plus you forgot, I still have the name tag."

As Ethan opened up his hand and showed Logan the Benjamin Jackson name tag Logan grabbed his chest. "Thank God! For a moment there I thought I would have to save your butt again."

Ethan, dumbfounded, "What you mean you would have to save my butt again? You keep on forgetting that I am the one who saves your little scrawny tail."

Logan laughed, "Well! We save each other. Just be careful and safe." Logan stoped at the front of the door again and then turned around. "Hey, Ethan! I do love you man and you better not tell no one, I said that either, or I will hang you on that flag pole, Ethan. I am not playing with you man." Ethan slowly turned around and walked away. "Hey! Ethan damn it, didn't you hear me?"

Ethan kept on walking, "Yeah, yeah I hear you." He walked into his classroom, with a big smile on his face.

Later that afternoon, the Matthew brothers had decided to try looking for Ms. Cooper. As they met each other in the lunchroom Logan approached Ethan. "Well I'm going to look behind the stove and you look in the refrigerator."

Ethan replied with a frown upon his face, "Logan, why would I check behind the stove when there are hotplate plug up everywhere?"

Logan thought, one finger on his bottom lip. "Oh damn! My bag. Well, check up under the table."

Ethan yelled out once again, "Logan! She is not going to be under no damn table. Look!" He waved his hand underneath the table.

Logan hunched his shoulders, "Well, hell, I don't know where to look."

Ethan put his hand over his face and shook his head. Then he lifted his head up and faced Logan. "Why are we here?"

Logan stopped and turned to look at Ethan, "To find Ms. Cooper, what else?"

Ethan had started to laugh, "... and you really think she is going to be in here, Logan. Now I know I am the smart one. We are in the freaking lunchroom, for crying out loud. Next you will be telling me to go and check the deep freezer."

As Ethan walked over to the deep freezer and opened it up. He still faced Logan, to whom he was talking. Logan peeked his head around Ethan, and his eyes got big and bright. "What are you looking at?" He turned to look at what Logan was staring at. Ethan looked back, he quickly slammed the deep freezer door with his mouth open, long before he was ready to say something. "I know that wasn't Ms. Cooper, was it?" He gestured with one finger in the air, and his mouth lay wide open. "Please tell me that... that body in that freezer... is not our math teacher!"

Logan noded his head. Ethan opened up the freezer once more to see if that was really Ms. Cooper. Then for a long time they looked from Ms. Cooper to each other.

Logan turned to face Ethan. "What are we going to do if anyone sees her in this freeze? They're going to think that we killed her."

Ethan kept on pacing back and forth. "Not if we get rid of the body just like we did with Mr. Jackson." Logan's looks at Ethan took on a stranger image.

"What, you want to dig a hold in the lunchroom floor? You have to come up with a better plan than that, big bro..."

Ethan put both of his hands on his head and rocked back and forth while pacing up and down the lunchroom floor. Logan's head turned back and forth, as Ethan kept on pacing. "Oh Okay," Logan grabbed Ethan by the arm, "Look I'm going to help you get out of this one this time, but from now on you have to help me get rid of this damn ghost that is killing everyone."

Ethan had stopped pacing as he brought one hand down slowly. "Come again? You help who? I believe that I was the one who told you how to get rid of that old man. The more they went back and forth with one another the less they paid attention to what was going on. The security guard was going down the hallway to make his rounds.

Logan had closed his mouth and looked at Ethan weirdly. "Shhh. I think I hear someone coming!"

Ethan made an uncomfortable face in reaction. "You don't hear anything. You are just trying to get out of this discussion that we are having."

Logan rolled his eyes at Ethan. "Will you shut up? I do hear someone coming." As the lunchroom had gotten quiet, all they could hear were heavy footsteps. The Matthew brothers looked at one another as they pursed their lips. They hoped that the footsteps that they were hearing were not those of the ghost of Mr. Benjamin Jackson.

# Chapter 13

As the footsteps drew closer, Logan and Ethan still looked at one another. "Do you think that's him?"

Logan's only reply for Ethan came as "Shhh! You are being too loud." Then he searched the space. "Come on let's hide behind this counter."

When the footsteps seemed right upon them the security guard yelled out, "Hey is anyone there?"

Logan noted to Ethan, "That's Mr. Simondale!" And they both jumped up from behind the counter.

Mr. Simondale turned around. "What are you boys doing in here, aren't you supposed to be in class?"

The Matthew brothers looked at one another, then looked back at Mr. Simondale. Logan, yelled out, "Uhh... Well, we are in here looking for our math book so we can go to Ms. Cooper's. Yeah,

*Linda Spence Howard*

we have to look for it in here because she will be very upset... if we come to class without it." Ethan looked at Logan with his head turned sideways, wearing a frown as if he could punch Logan right at the top of his head.

Mr. Simondale walked over to the Matthew brothers. "Well hurry up and get your things and get back to class. Or I'll make sure that you two will be sent home for a couple of days. I have been watching you two, and you boys do nothing but keep trouble going all around this school."

Ethan looked back at Mr. Simondale and started to reply more than actually ask, "What the ..."

Logan put his hand over Ethan's mouth. "Yes, we are getting ready to leave now." As they both headed out of the lunchroom. Logan stopped and turned around to look at Ethan. We just have to come back later on when the school is closed.

Ethan stepped back from Logan and looked at him up and down. "You have lost your damn mind...you know that? I'm not coming back to break into no school to put a dead teacher in the ground."

Logan said, "Okay then, well I guess I'll have to visit you in jail then...

Ethan's facial expression changed. "Okay! What time do you want me here?"

Logan smiled and they walked away, headed back to class. John stepped from around the counter in the lunchroom food center. He peered around to make sure that no one had seen him, then, all of a sudden a wind had started blow with a little chill. John looked all around the lunchroom trying to figure out where this cool wind is coming from. The brief distraction did not deter him from snooping around and try to find out why the Matthew brothers were looking for their math book here. He thought to himself, 'Now why would they come into a lunchroom to look for a math book?' The more he thought about it, the more it turned from cool to colder. 'Man, why is it so cool in here? I know it's a lunchroom and everything... but my god. Does it have to be this cold?'

As John got closer to the freezer he started to smell something horrible. John pulled the collar of his shirt over his nose. He thought to himself, 'My god did the lunch lady forget to clean up and take the trash out? It smells like S-H-I-T in here. Man, I can't take this horrible smell, I just have to come back when that smell leaves.'

As John was getting ready to leave the lunchroom Mr. Simondale was headed back down the hallway again for another check. 'Oh shit!' John jumped back into the lunchroom, "where the hell did he come from. Now how am I going to get out of here? With that smell and Mr. Simondale on my trail, man this is turning out to be the worst day ever.' Mr. Simondale had come to the end of the hall, then turned around. 'Man, I thought he would never leave!' John quickly ran back down the hallway to his class, but when he turned the corner Mr. Simondale was standing right in front of the classroom.

As the security guard turned around John ran smack dead into him, "And may I ask what are you doing out of your classroom?

John stoped in his tracks, "I want to go to the bathroom."

Mr. Simondale looked him up and down. Then he looked down at John's hands, "Where is your hall pass at son, and you better not be lying to me either?"

John thought to himself, "Now, how am I going to get out of this big lie? Think John...think.' The more he tried to think the more it seemed the smell leaked off of his clothes.

Mr. Simondale looked at John and fell back a step. "What is that smell on you kid? You smell like you just came from out of the gutter."

It was all John could do to look down at his clothes. Looking back at the security guard he started, "Well, if you let me go and call my parents I..." John had gotten stuck with the lie he was trying to make up about the smell he had into his clothes.

The security guard kept on backing back. "Please just leave, you smell horrible. As matter of fact... stay home until you get that smell off of you."

John glanced back at Mr. Simondale as he left and smiled. John ran past the Matthew brothers as the hall bell rang. Ethan and Logan had stopped and turned around to look at one another. "Was that John that ran past us?"

Ethan looked and then covered his nose. "Yeah, but what the hell type of cologne he got on? That mess stinks."

Logan frowned and then answered back, "Man, I don't think this no cologne smell."

They turned up towards the lunchroom. Ethan slowed and then looked back at Logan, pointing to the lunchroom. "Is that Ms. Cooper smelling like that? She is coming out of the freezer." They had to was cover their noses up with their shirts to go on.

Logan turned and looked at Ethan, "What if someone thinks that we killed Ms. Cooper and the old man."

Ethan turned and looked at Logan with his hand still covering his nose. "What the hell are you talking about? All I know is that this smell is going to have everyone sick to their stomach, if we don't hurry up and move that body."

Logan frowned at Ethan. "Wait... the hell, one min! You mean to tell me that we have to move a body of someone I didn't even kill and she stinks? No! The hell I ain't. And furthermore, you didn't want to help me when the old man died. So no... I'm not going back to that lunchroom and help move a darn thing." As the security guard was coming down the hallway, Logan looked back at Ethan with a pale complexion. Then, as he saw Mr. Simondale coming ever closer, Logan turned back to Ethan again. "Man, you better come on so we can move this body in this lunchroom." All Ethan could do was look and shake his head.

Then he looked at Logan quizzically. Logan responded with, "What's wrong, why are you looking like that?"

Ethan turned around and replied, "I think John knows what's in that freezer. That's why that smell was on him."

Logan steps back to regard Ethan with a weird look. "No, he couldn't have known about Ms. Cooper being in that freeze unless he went snooping around to find out what we know about that ghost." They spent a moment trying to figure out how to move Ms. Cooper before Ethan turned and looked at the fire alarm. With a big smile on his face he looked back at Logan. "Are you thinking what I'm thinking?"

Logan had started to step back, "No! I'm not and if you think that I'm going..." Before Logan could get the rest of the words out of his mouth Ethan had already pulled the fire alarm down. Logan looked at Ethan with surprise. "What the hell you do that for?"

Ethan had started looking around to see if any of the students or teachers were heading out of the building. "You do want to move Ms. Cooper's body don't you? This is our chance to move it while everyone is outside."

Logan turned and looked back and forth to make sure no one was coming. However, there was one person he forgot to check out... Mr. Simondale the security guard. As they both ran into the lunchroom to get Ms. Cooper out of the freezer, all they could smell was old dried-up blood and raw meat.

*Linda Spence Howard*

"Okay Logan, I'm going to need you to open the freezer and pull Ms. Cooper out."

Logan looked at him cockeyed, "Why the hell you always volunteering me?"

Ethan shook his head at Logan. "Because I did the last one. Remember?"

"That doesn't mean anything," Logan shot back.

Ethan walked a step toward Logan, "Get over there!" He hissed as he pointed to the freezer where Ms. Cooper was. Logan only looked for a long moment.

"Well, you don't have to holler, damn it. I'm going." Thus Logan decided to pull Ms. Cooper out of the freezer. As he was opening it to pull Ms. Cooper out he saw Mr. Benjamin Jackson laying next to her. Logan hurriedly shut the freezer and looked at Ethan.

"What's wrong, Logan, why did you slam the freezer like you saw..." by the look in Logan's eyes Ethan knew Logan had just seen the ghost of Mr. Benjamin Jackson.

# Chapter 14

Logan stood there with his hand on the freezer pushing down as tightly as he could. Ethan looked back at the lunchroom door hoping no would see them. "Logan," he whispered sharply, "now what are we going to do?"

Logan swiveled his head to face Ethan with a frown. "We? What do you mean we? I'm over here holding on to a deep freezer with a dead body and a crazy ass ghost that will not leave me the hell alone, and you got a nerve to ask what are we going to do?"

Ethan took a deep breath in, "Okay. Well you can open up the freezer and see if the ghost is still there."

Logan rolled his eyes then squinched them tightly as he turned his head. "You know, I am getting a little sick and tired of you telling me how and when I should do things."

Ethan took another deep breath and held his head up straight, "Well, Logan with the master plan, please tell me how we are going to get a dead body, and a wandering ghost out of the lunchroom."

Logan squinched his eyes a little more tighter. "I don't know, but we need to come up with something fast because that fire alarm is not going to stay on forever, Mr. Ethan." As they went back and forth with one another they failed to notice that Mr. Jackson was slowly creeping out of the freezer.

Ethan had stopped talking and looked over Logan's shoulder with his eyes widening. Logan thought he was looking at Ethan to return his strange stare. "What the hell is wrong with you?" Logan turned around to see what Ethan was looking at. All of his view was filled with Mr. Jackson standing right in front of him. "Oh Shit!" He backed up to make a run for it. Logan yelled behind him, "Why the hell you didn't tell me that thing came out of the freeze, Jackass?!"

They both ran down the hallway trying to get away from the ghost of who bellowed out, "I want my revenge, I want your soul now!" The voice continued to get louder. The Matthew brothers kept on running until Ethan had tripped over his feet and fell to the ground.

Logan stopped and turned around to run back to help Ethan off the floor. "Come on..." It started to seem that the more they ran the closer Mr. Jackson got. Logan stopped, "Hey, maybe if we ran outside he wouldn't come after us." Ethan stopped running, too, holding on to his chest as he bent over to catch his breath.

He looked up at Logan. "You really think this damn ghost cares about us going outside? He's trying to kill us, Logan. What part you don't understand: The killing part, or you're just straight dumb? Which one Logan, huh? Please tell me. I got to know."

Logan grabbed Ethan, "Come on this way," as they ran into the janitorial closet.

Pressed face to face Ethan asked, "Is this the best that you can come up with? I at least thought you were going to say let's…"

Logan covered Ethan's mouth with his hand. "Will you shut up, before this thing gets the both of us?"

With Ethan and Logan's terse whispering the ghost of Benjamin Jackson could hear their hiding place. So, as the fire alarm finally completely stopped, everyone began entering back into the school building. Mr. Simondale had continued doing his rounds by going into the classrooms. As he came across a shadow that he thought he had seen Mr. Simondale turned and looked with his flashlight back at a door he had walked by before. Checking an English room to make sure that everything was in place as they should be he felt a big gust of cold wind. Mr. Simondale shivered at the chill. 'Man, what in the world did that cold air came from? Oh well,' he brushed it off as he continued to himself, 'you know it stays cold in this school.' As Mr. Simondale went to walk out of the classroom, the door slammed and locked. "What in God's green Earth is going on here?" He tried to reach for the door handle, but as far as he could see it had started to melt. Mr. Simondale started to yell, "Help! Someone help me, please! I can't get out of here!" The walls had started to turn red like blood that came down thick and heavy. He stepped back and looked, big and wide-eyed, there seemed no way out. His hollering had made his voice squeak. Next Mr. Jackson slowly came down one wall and then walked over to Mr. Simondale, who had backed up to a wall and now slid down it to the floor. As he looked up at Mr. Jackson's pale black dusty face the latter reached his hand out and wrapped his whole hand around Mr. Simondale's face. He took the last breath that Mr. Simondale had in his body, leaving the security guard flat on the classroom floor.

The Matthew brothers started to come out of the janitor closet in the hallway and agreed as they looked around to make sure that no one would see them. "Okay all we have to do now is watch out for Mr. Simondale."

"You know he doesn't like us, so be careful." As they started to blend in with everyone in the hallway, Ethan stopped and turned around to look back at Logan. "Does it feel kinda of weird to you, that you don't see Mr. Simondale anywhere in the building?"

Logan kept on walking, looking around to see if he could find Mr. Simondale. "Yeah! That is kind of strange – he normally be in the hallway telling you 'Get back to class,' or 'You're moving too slow,' something."

While they were looking for the security guard Ethan noticed that all the students were cutting class and running in the hallway. Ethan turns to Logan, "Yeah, something is not right here. Where is Mr. Simondale at?" Immediately, as if in answer, they hear one of the teachers screaming out loud. She ran back out of her classroom as if she had seen the ghost herself. The Matthew brothers went running down the hallway as fast as they could. By the time they got there Mr. Simondale's body had disappeared. Everyone that had seen it looked around at one another.

"Do you think that Mrs. Johnson has lost her mind?" One of the other students had looked over to ask Logan. He turned around to looked back at the young lady and said, "No, She knows exactly what she saw." The Matthew brothers looked at one another and shook their heads knowingly.

# Chapter 15

Mrs. K. Johnson came running back into the classroom wondering as to where the body of Mr. Simondale had vanished. She looked all around the room. Silently she hoped that no one would think that she was losing her mind because of what she saw. Mrs. Johnson turned and looked back at the Matthew brothers. "I know I saw his body right there – on that floor." She pointed down with her hand shaking. The more she looked at the floor the more she wondered if she had been hallucinating. "This can't be right, he was laying on the floor a minute ago." Everyone just started to stare at her and she started to back further into the room while rubbing her hands through her hair.

Ethan took Mrs. K. Johnson by the hand. "I know you might have thought that you saw Mr. Simondale, but there is no one there now." As he was still leading her by the hand towards a chair Logan turned and looked at Ethan as if he had lost his mind.

Logan pulled Ethan by the arm, "Are you insane? You know damn well she saw that body," as he whispered sharply to Ethan the older boy, who looked up at Logan

"Yes, I know she saw Mr. Simondale laying there on the floor, but if she continues to act like she is insane, they're going to think she is."

Logan shook his head. "Now what are we going to do? We have one dead body, which I have to remind you is Ms. Cooper and now we have a missing body that we don't know where to look for..." The more Logan would talk and get upset, the more his hands started to sweat.

Ethan looked down at Logan's hands. "Try to calm down before you have everyone looking at you."

Logan looked down at his hands and began to wipe them on his pants. "Well come on," he said sternly, "the last bell is about to ring for the day and we still haven't figured out... well, anything." Logan turned to Ethan, "What if we take Mrs. Johnson with us home until this whole thing blows over?"

Ethan rolled his head back, "Are you crazy?! Because if you are I can take you straight to the nurse's office right now!" Logan frowned as if he wanted to kick Ethan right in his knee caps.

"No, forget it let's go home. And besides, we still have to find Mr. Haywood and make sure he didn't go to the police and tell them anything."

Ethan's eyes widened, "Oh yeah, I forgot all about Mr. Haywood. Dag!"

Now it was Logan's turn to roll his head at Ethan and exclaim, "How the hell you forget about Mr. Haywood? We did kill his brother, remember?" Logan took a deep breath in and whispered to himself as he walked away, 'How the hell you forget, yeah right."

As they both headed out of the school doors. Mrs. K. Johnson looked over at the Matthew brothers still rubbing her hands through her hair. Logan turned and looked back at her and he continued thinking to himself, 'Man, I wish I could take you home with me my love, but I can't,' as the bell rang for dismissal Logan thought he noticed the big, black shadow behind Mrs. Johnson. Logan began to run out of the building as fast as his legs could take him.

Ethan turned and looked back to see what Logan was running from. "What the...?" escaped his mouth as a gust of wind came by. Ethan felt the cold air as if it had come off Logan's clothes when he fled past. "Logan what the hell is wrong with you, and why are you running out of the building like that? You know that there is no running in the building, jerk!"

Logan stopped as he got next to their car. "You didn't see that black shadow that's behind Mrs. Johnson?"

Ethan turned and looked all around the school yard. "Are you sure you saw a black shadow behind Mrs. Johnson?" Ethan asking made Logan seem even more scared.

"Yes, man! I saw it again. Please, Ethan, don't think I'm going crazy, Okay... That thing was behind her and if we don't get her out of there, that thing is going to kill her!"

Ethan waved his hand back and forth at Logan, "Okay, Okay, we can go, and we'll get her out of there, but you have to promise me that when I go in there you will not let her know about our little secret, Okay."

Logan, trying to catch his breath, "Yeah, I won't say a word. Hey, what are we going to do about Ms. Cooper in the freeze?"

Ethan stopped and turned back, "I don't know, but for now, we have to remove Mrs. Johnson before the principal ends up calling the cops.

Later on that night Ethan took Mrs. Johnson up to Logan's room. Logan looked at Ethan and then back at the teacher as they went up the stairs. "Hey man," Logan whispers over Ethan's shoulder, "why does she have to have my room?

Ethan stopped at the top of the stairs and turned around. "Because this was your idea to bring her home. And another thing, you'd better hope that mom and dad don't find out what you have done, 'cause I can't keep bailing you out of your messes that you keep on creating."

Logan scowled and walked away. As a knock hit the front door Ethan and Logan looked at one another. 'Who could that be at this time of the day?' Logan went to open the door but Ethan yelled out

"Wait, Logan we don't know who or what it could be?"

Logan looked up the stairs, "So what do you want me to do, just let them knock, or should I go and answer it, your highness?"

Ethan looked down the stairs, "Ha ha, very funny, Logan." Ethan came running down the stairs to see who was at the door. The knock had started to get louder, and a man and a woman's voice had started to speak.

Logan turned to Ethan, "Hey, I think that's mom and dad."

Ethan thought and then replied, "No way, they're not supposed to be back until next week." Logan turned and looked back at Ethan with an expression on his face that told his brother he was getting on his last nerve.

Logan went to open the door, but Ethan ran and slammed it back. Logan turned his head sideways to look at Ethan, "What the hell is wrong with you. That's mom and dad, you idiot!" Logan tried to open the door once again. Ethan turned pressed it shut again.

"Look, you keep forgetting that Mrs. Johnson is upstairs, butt wipe, and for another thing; How do we know for sure that's our parents?"

Logan stepped back, "You know you might be right..." but the smile on his face said he could care less., and he opened the front door. All they could see out there was a mass of smokey, gray clouds. Logan turned and looked at Ethan, "What the hell?!" With his mouth open as wide as it could go. Ethan walks from behind Logan and stared out the front door.

"I told you, you idiot, that... that thing was going to be out there!" Ethan went to shut the front door, but suddenly Mr. Haywood walked through the heavy, gray clouds. He pushed the door the rest of the way open to step inside.

"Hey, wait a minute, you didn't forget about me, now did you?"

Ethan caught the door in it's swing, his eyes lit up like a christmas tree. "Man, I'm so happy to see you, buddy, old pal."

Logan stood back, folding his arms while looking at Ethan with a frown on his face. "You do know we still have Mrs. Johnson up stairs right, Ethan?" He kept looking at Ethan trying to give him visible reminders about Mrs. K. Johnson. Mr. Haywood strode into the house and Logan nodded his head at Ethan in the direction of upstairs. Through tight lips he whispered, "You can't let him in here right now Ethan; we still have our English teacher upstairs. What are you thinking? If he sees her we are all going to be in big trouble, and this time I'm not going to take the fall, Mr. I-know-everything."

Ethan spat back, "What are you so up-tight about? If Mr. Haywood sees Mrs. Johnson we'll just tell him that she is here to help us with our English homework, duh."

Logan looked at Ethan and then back at Mr. Haywood. "This had better work, 'cause if it..." All of the sudden the lights started to dim and flicker. Everyone looked around at one another, and then Mrs. Johnson came running down the stairs. "It's here! It's here, that thing is going to kill me!"

Mr. Haywood turned to Logan, "Who she, and where did she come from?"

Ethan pulled Mr. Haywood by the arm, "Well, I think you need to help me down in the basement again, Mr. Haywood."

The old man turned and started to back up. "Oh no"! I'm not going back down there anymore. You know exactly what happened the last time we went down there."

Mrs. Johnson took a step, looking at Mr. Haywood strangely, "What happened the last time... and can someone please tell me what is going on before I lose my ever-loving mind?"

The Matthew brothers looked at one another, then back at Mr. Haywood, and Mrs. Johnson. Logan put his hand on her shoulder, "I know we haven't told you everything, but I promise when the time is right. I will tell you everything, Okay? But for now we have to deal with an unwanted ghost that just will not leave me or my brother alone." Then he turned and looked at Mr. Haywood and asked, "Are you going to help us take down this crazy ghost? Because if you're not going to help us then you're just going be in our way."

# Chapter 16

Mr. Haywood looked quizzically at both of the Matthew brothers. "But why should I help you take down my brother... when you kill him on purpose. You really thought that I was going to go and get help for you, after what you have done. You gotta be crazy." He showed a big, crazy grin. Logan turned and looked back at Ethan, then at Mrs. Johnson. Mr. Haywood walked toward Mrs. Johnson and reached for her arm. She snatched her arm back, and at the same time Logan pushed her toward the kitchen so she could get away. "Don't think that I won't find you boys and whatever her name is... you forgot you showed me all of your hiding spots."

As Mr. Haywood began to walk toward the kitchen he heard strange sounds coming from the dining room, so he turned and headed that way. There he noticed that the window was open. "Well... well... well... I know you don't think that you want me to know that you went out of the window, now do you?" Mr. Haywood began to walk over to the open window when, all of the sudden, Ethan came running behind him with a candlestick in his hand. Ethan hit Mr. Haywood over the head with it as hard as he could. Mr. Haywood stumbled. Ethan came down once more and hit him again. This time Mr. Haywood fell to the floor. Ethan took the candlestick and nudged him on the side. Mr. Haywood laid there playing as if he was dead. As Ethan turned to walk away the old man grabbed him by the ankle holding on as if for dear life.

Ethan fell to the floor, then he kicked and crawled trying to get away from Mr. Haywood. Ethan yelled out, "Logan, help me! He won't let me go!" Logan and Mrs. Johnson came running into the dining area, and looked down at Ethan while struggled to get away.

Mrs. Johnson began to pull Ethan by his arms, but Mr. Haywood still had a tight grip on his legs. It seemed the more she pulled the tighter his hold. "Let him go, you damned creep."

Logan stopped to look at Mrs. Johnson, then at Ethan. The look on his face said he couldn't believe that his English teacher had just cussed. Logan looked around the room to see if he could find something with which he could hit Mr. Haywood. Momentarily he saw the candlestick next to Ethan, Logan picks up the golden heavy candlestick and started to strike Mr. Haywood over and over again.

The impacts made Mr. Haywood let Ethan go, finally. Ethan hurriedly pushed himself off the floor. He launched himself towards the wall to put his back against. The Matthew brothers and Mrs. K. Johnson all looked at one another, all three were out of breath and holding their chests. Mr. Haywood's body had started to transform into that of Mr. Benjamin Jackson. Logan looked over at Ethan. "Now what are we going to do with this body?" While Logan yelled 'what are we going to do' Ethan paced back and forth rubbing his hands through his hair. Logan kept on hollering until

Ethan yelled out, "Damn Logan, Give me a second! I'm trying to think of what to do with him." The more he paced the more nervous he got.

Mrs. Johnson chimed in, "I know what we can do with him." Ethan stopped pacing and looked expectantly at her.

"Okay... what can we do with this dingbat that is on my floor?"

Mrs. Johnson replied, "We can drive him out into the woods and dump his body as if someone had done a hit and run."

Both of the Matthew brothers turned to look at one another. "Okay, so whose car are we going to use?"

Logan turned and looked back at Mrs. Johnson who added, "Well, We can use my car. That way, if we get stopped by the police. I can tell them that he is my husband, and you two boys are my sons."

Ethan regarded Mrs. Johnson. "Wait a minute. You've done this before haven't you?" he asked with his finger pointing at her.

All she did in reply was smile and say, "Now boys, don't get the wrong idea about little old Mrs. Johnson, you hear. All I'm trying to do is help you boys out so you won't be in any trouble. First things first; we have to make sure he is not breathing., then... Oh, I forgot – he is my real husband."

Logan and Ethan's eyes had started to widen as they began to back slowly out of the dining room.

Mrs. K. Johnson turned around to look at the Matthew brothers with a smile on her face. "Wait boys, I can help you get rid of the body, but you have to trust me. Honestly, I won't tell a soul what happened tonight, but you will have to help me get rid of Mr. Haywood. Deal?"

Logan walked back in the dining room area and pointed down, "So you mean to tell me that ... this crazy old man ... is your husband, and you didn't say anything to us at all. I thought we could trust you Mrs. Johnson, but I see that we can't."

Ethan walked towards Mrs. Johnson and Logan. "Wait a minute Logan. She gave us her word that she wouldn't tell no one and so far she has done that. So come on, give her a chance. And besides, we need all the help we can get right now. If she decides to go to the police and tell, then she is in just as much trouble as we are. So stop trying to be Mr. Hard-ass, and help us move this body."

Logan frowned and looked at them for a long time before he walked over toward where Mr. Haywood was laying. "Don't we need some tape and rope to tie him up?"

Mrs. K. Johnson and Ethan looked at one another. "Yeah, that would be a good idea, thanks Logan." Logan rolled his eyes as if the both of them were getting on his last nerve.

Ethan had gone into the kitchen to get the duct tape and rope, when all of the sudden the lights started to blink off and on. Ethan stopped in the middle of the kitchen floor and looked around, back and forth. The more he moved the more the lights flickered. "Okay, Mr. Benjamin Jackson, I know you here, so go on. I don't have time for you right now, and besides, we have your brother."

Then the lights went completely out, leaving Ethan to fumble his way around the kitchen to find a flashlight. Then he thought to himself, 'What if I call both of them in here to help me?' As he started to call Logan's and Mrs. Johnson's names Mr. Benjamin Jackson's black shadow started to appear. All around the kitchen he could see the face of an old man wearing an overall jumper. Ethan's eyes watered as he tried to call out Logan's name, but there was no sound coming. Ethan grabbed at his throat and held tightly trying to scream out Logan's name, but all he could hear was silence and the swirling dust. Ethan began to knock over all the pots and pans and even swept the silverware off the counter. Mrs. Johnson and Logan came rushing into the kitchen. However, by the time they got there it was totally dark.

Logan yelled out Ethan's name, "Hey Ethan, man, where are you? I can't see a thing in here!" Mrs. Johnson went to switch on the light, but there was no light coming on. Ethan tried again to knock over things but it was no use – they could neither see nor hear him. Still trying to yell out Logan's name, he could see Mr. Jackson standing right in front of him.

Logan went to stick his hand out so that Ethan could feel him. "Okay, Ethan I have my hand out. Tell me if you can feel my hand!"

One thing Logan didn't tell Ethan to do was kick him. "Ouch! What you kick me for?"

Ethan then pulled Logan toward him and held on tight. "Okay, Okay... I got you. Please let me go. You don't have to hold on to me that darn tight. Besides, why are you holding on to me like this?" Ethan had buried his face into Logan's chest and then let out a big cry.

By the time Ethan let out that sound the lights came back on.

"What is wrong with you? All I did was send you in here to find some duct tape and rope, and you want to cry about that... Really, Ethan?"

When Ethan got himself together he replied, "No, you idiot... he was here in the kitchen with me. He had turned out all the lights, and he took my voice."

Mrs. Johnson peered at the Matthew brothers with a strange look. "Wait, who took your voice and turned out the lights?"

Ethan turned to answer her with a scared look on his face, "Mr. Benjamin Jackson, that's who."

*Linda Spence Howard*

Mrs. Johnson just looked at him a moment. "Benjamin who's that?"

Logan addressed them both, "Okay, right now we have to get back into the dining room area to tie Mr. Haywood up. I know y'all didn't forget about him..."

They ran into the dining area where Mr. Haywood had been, but by the time they got there Mr. Haywood had vanished.

# Chapter 17

"Now what are we going to do? We have a ghost that will not leave us alone, Mr. Haywood is now on the loose – and, by the way, when did he become your husband? I thought this was our plan to get rid of him, not a game about your husband."

Mrs. K. Johnson had stepped back showing a shocked expression. "Boys, I know I haven't been honest with you from day one, yes Mr. Haywood is my husband, and yes, I have been trying to get a divorce. From the looks of things, however, he's not trying to give me one. He never told me anything about his family. The more I would ask, the more he would get mad and storm out."

Logan returned her looks. "Wait, you mean to tell me that you don't know anything about this man, and you still married him? How the heck did you become a school teacher?"

*Linda Spence Howard*

Mrs. Johnson shot back at Logan "I beg your pardon?! Excuse me!"

Ethan had walked in-between Mrs. Johnson and Logan and put his arms out in the distance between them, "Look, you two, we still have to find this ghost and whatever he is to you. So I suggest the both of you quit fighting, and let's move on. We all have a big day tomorrow at school. So I suggest both of you get along now."

As they all got stepped outside look for Mr. Haywood the front door swung closed and locked everyone out. Ethan went to try to turn the knob, but it wouldn't turn. "I think it's stuck, it won't turn." Ethan and Logan banged on the front door as loudly as they could.

Mrs. Johnson yelled out, "What are you doing? Apparently the door is locked from the inside, and neither of you have your key, do you?" Ethan and Logan turned and looked at one another, then back at Mrs. Johnson.

"No, we left it on the coffee table." Ethan started rubbing his head again, "Dag man, I left the name tag on the table, too."

Logan turned accusingly on Ethan. "You did what? What do you mean, you left the name tag on the table? I told you to keep it on you at all times, you big jerk."

As Ethan and Logan debated back and forth, Mrs. Johnson stepped back and put her two fingers in her mouth whistled shrilly. Logan and Ethan stopped arguing. As they turned to face her she admonished them. "Are you two done yet? Now, one of you boys go around the side of the house and climb through the window."

"You can do it..." Logan and Ethan started arguing again until Mrs. Johnson slowly put her two fingers back to her mouth, but by the time she went to whistle, Logan stopped her. "Okay, I'll go, for crying out loud I'll do it." Logan walked around the side of the house to try and open up the front room window. Just then he looked down and saw two boot footprint in the flower bed. Logan bent down to see whose footprints they were, but then they started to disappear. Logan shoot his head in disbelief, 'Now I know that I just saw two footprints on this ground. What the hell is going on around here?' Logan started to look all around to see if anyone was outside besides him. 'Okay well, I don't see anyone, so I'll just go climb through the window.' Logan jumped up to and then through the window when all of sudden Logan felt someone pulling him by his legs. Logan kicked and squirmed his way through the window. When he fell to the dining room floor, Logan scrambled his way to the front door.

When Logan opened the front door Ethan turned and asked blithely, "What took you so long to open up the door?"

Logan turned and looked first at Mrs. Johnson, then at his brother. "Well, I had a little trouble getting in, and beside I saw two footprints in the flower bed."

Ethan leaned his head over and looked at Logan with a curious look. "What you mean you saw two footprints in the flower bed? What does that have to do with you opening up the front door? So, who's were they?"

Logan put his hands together over his nose as if he was about to pray. "I don't know, but I do know someone else is watching us, so we have to be careful."

"Mrs. Johnson got the Matthew brothers attention. "What if it was Haywood? You do know he just escaped from out of here?" She paused, "Besides, which window did you come through to get in?"

Logan stepped back to look at her. "Why does that matter? All we know is that he got away, and we still have a ghost, and now two footprints in our mother's flower bed."

Mrs. Johnson walked in front of Logan and with a high pitch coming from her voice, "Were you listening to anything I just asked? He just got away through the window that you had just crawled into. They are his footprints, you idiot."

Logan stepped back from the angry English teacher. "Who do you think you are talking to like that? And furthermore, I'm not an idiot, you old bat."

Ethan took a deep breath in. "Will you two cut it out just for one second?! Please! We still have to find Mr. Haywood, and we have to try to kill that damned ghost, but if you two do not quit arguing we are never going to get anything done."

Logan raised his hand and looked at Ethan. "May I ask a question?" Ethan looked at Logan with a frown on his face.

"What is it, and why the hell you got your hand up in the air like you in third grade or something?"

"Well, all I wanted to say is the ghost you are talking about, Mr. Ethan, he is dead. Remember, jackass, the cemetery..."

Ethan turned back to Logan with his eyes squinting tightly.

"Look, I don't have time to be arguing back and forth with you or Mrs. Johnson like I'm some crazy idiot."

Mrs. Johnson stepped between them and looked back and forth at both of the Matthew brothers. "First of all, I'm not going to be fussing with two uneducated clowns that think they saw a ghost!"

Logan laughed, "Uneducated, my dear, let me get this straight. A minute ago I could have sworn that you saw the same damn ghost that we did. Now who's the uneducated one, you damn bat?"

Mrs. Johnson went on to say something else but Ethan had cut her off.

"Look, you two, I don't have time for this crap right now. Logan, I need you to go and get the name tag off the coffee table, and Mrs. Johnson I need you to start up the car."

Now they both looked at him. "And what are you going to be doing Mr.-I'm-giving-all-of-the-directions?"

Ethan took another deep breath in, "I'm going to be holding the door open, so it won't shut again, thank you Mr. and Mrs. President."

They both looked at Ethan while he walked away. They both rolled their eyes at him before going about their assignments. "Who the hell does he think he is?" Logan mumbled under his breath while still looking at him, "You Jack Nicholson looking ass..."

Ethan whipped around at Logan. "I heard that."

Logan stopped at the front door. "Good! I wanted you to hear it!"

Ethan yelled back at Logan. "Will you just get the damn name tag and come back here so we can find Mr. Haywood?"

Logan came stepping back into the front door as if he wasn't worried about Mr. Haywood or Mr. Benjamin Jackson. Ethan snatched the name tag out of his hand. "Give me that. You started to get on my last nerve, you know that?"

All Logan could do was smile and walk past his brother with his head up in the air. Ethan glared back at Logan. "You think this is all a game, don't you?"

Logan returned the looks back at Ethan and walked toward him. "Do I think this is a game? Hell No! I don't think this is a game! You forgot, big brother, the ghost was in me and I almost died. Did you forget that brother?"

Ethan grabbed Logan by the arm. "No man I didn't forget it, but you are acting like you don't have a care in your body whether this ghost kills us or not. That's all I'm saying."

As the Matthew brothers discussion turned into a stare-down, Mrs. Johnson cames driving up to the house. "Well come on.

Let's go find this ghost and kill Haywood before he decides he wants to kill us."

# Chapter 18

Once they all got settled into the car they looked forward to find Mr. Jackson was standing right in front of them. Mrs. Johnson saw only a man in a black overall jean jumper as she had not met him before this night. However she started to scream out, "There he is again!"

Logan first looked at Mrs. Johnson, "Oh no! We are not doing that again," with a look on his face as if he could care less.

"No, look," As Mrs. Johnson pointed toward the windshield Logan, mouth hanging open, could see what made Mrs. Johnson scream. "Oh my god!" Logan stared at Mr. Jackson with the shock of his life.

Ethan jumped in the front seat slamming his foot down on the gas pedal. Ethan hollered out, "Let's go." As the car lurched backwards Mr. Benjamin Jackson started to walk at a slow pace to follow.

Mrs. Johnson was still yelling and screaming, "He is going to kill us! What do we do?"

Ethan straightened the car to drive away fast. Mr. Jackson continued walking at a slow pace behind them.

Logan turned and looked at Ethan, "Where the hell did he come from?!"

Ethan faced back to Logan. "I don't know, but we need to go back to the cemetery. We need to make sure that no one has dug up his body."

Logan replied wide-eyed and gaping at Ethan, "Are you crazy?! I'm not going back into that cemetery this time of the night! You got to be out of your damned mind, thinking I'm going back in..."

Before Logan could finish his sentence Mrs. Johnson added, "I think we do need to go back to the Cemetery and make sure."

Logan leaned his head back exclaiming, "I don't care what you think, Mrs. I didn't see no Mrs.-educated-ghost."

Mrs. Johnson frowned at Logan, "What Ever, anyhow, like he said we do need to make sure that no one has dug up his body. Haywood or someone, or anyone..."

Logan glared back at her. "You know you are starting to get on my last damn nerves. You know that?" With a low tone in his voice.

All Mrs. Johnson simply slid over toward the back seat car door. As they pulled up to the cemetery they noticed that the grave was still covered with dirt. Logan and Ethan stepped out of the car while Mrs. Johnson stayed in. They both walked over toward Mr. Benjamin Jackson's covered, undisturbed grave. Logan looked up at Ethan. Then... if his grave is covered, then who the hell is that trying to kill us?"

Ethan turned to face Logan. "I don't know, but let's look around and make sure that this is the right spot that we put him in." As they started to walk around. Logan turned on the flashlight on his phone so they could see. Ethan examined Logan's light, "that little flashlight is not going to work out here in this dark. Do you know where we are Logan?"

Logan swung his head around at Ethan. "Yes I know where we are, smart ass. I'm the one who suggested that we don't come here but, oh no, you and Mrs.-I-know-everything wanted to come here."

Ethan had stopped walking and turned back to look at Logan with a frown, then a raised eyebrow and a lowering tone. "This is the wrong place for you to be mouthing off at me, else I will make sure you will stay out here all alone. So stop patronizing me, Logan"

Logan began to walk towards the other side of the cemetery. "You are crazy, you know that?"

Ethan turned back on Logan again with a straight face. "Stop playing with me"

Logan thought his brother had lost his mind.

As they searched for the grave the air started to change. Logan looked in Ethan's direction. "We never going to find this grave in the dark, Ethan, and It's starting to get a little nippy out here." he brought his jacket up towards his ears. Yet they kept on walking around the cemetery. Ethan noticed an older looking headstone.

"Hey, Logan, look!" his brother walked over toward the headstone and pointed his phone flashlight to the inscription. As the light shone on the headstone Ethan read. Then he looked up at Logan. "Does this say what I think it says?" Logan bent down closer to look at what was written on the headstone.

Ethan put his hands in his packet and remembered that he still had the name tag of Mr. Benjamin Jackson. He pulled it out and put it up against the headstone. There sat the same name as the name tag. The brothers turned and looked at one another agape. "Then who was that man that we were supposed to have put in the ground?" They ran back to the other grave. Ethan looked over at the car and noticed that Mrs. Johnson was not there. "Wait," as Ethan pointed to the car, "where is Mrs. Johnson at? Don't tell me that Mr. Jackson got her too!"

Logan looked over at the car and declared, "Good, he needed to get her."

Ethan looked incredulously at Logan. "Why would you say that? You're the one who suggested that she come alone with us."

Logan turned and rolled his eyes. "Yeah, I did... until she started to get on my last nerves. You know that lady thinks she knows everything."

Ethan leaned his head back in exasperation and then looked at Logan. "You do know that she is a school teacher, right?"

All Logan could do was look at him with his face scrunched up. "Whatevery! Look, we need to find all three of these psychopaths before they end up taking our souls. And, yes, I have a good feeling that this English teacher of ours is not telling us the truth about Mr. Haywood."

Ethan had started to walk toward the car. He looked up at Logan. "You really think she's in on this?"

Logan parted to walk towards the other side of the car. As he was leaning to get in he looked confidently at Ethan. "Yes, I think she is."

Mrs. Johnson suddenly ran up behind Logan with an iron pipe in her hand. As Ethan looked back at Logan his eyes widened. "Hey man, what's... Watch out, Logan!" Logan quickly turned around barely in time to see Mrs. Johnson rushing towards him.

As she swung the iron pipe at him, Logan ducked. Mrs. Johnson missed Logan's head by an inch. Logan turned fully around. "What the hell is wrong with you lady?"

Mrs. Johnson came at him again swinging the pipe again as hard as she could. Ethan came around the car behind Mrs. Johnson and tried to get the pipe out of her hands, but she turned and swung the pipe directly at his face. Both of the Matthew brothers had to make a run for it back towards the cemetery to try to hide.

Mrs. Johnson began to walk slowly into the cemetery right after the Matthew brothers. "I know you boys think that I want to hurt you, but all I want to do is take you to Mr. Benjamin Jackson so he can take your souls." The Matthew brothers hid behind a tall statue and look at one another. Mrs. Johnson steadily walked into the cemetery trying to find them.

Ethan whispered, "We need to make a run for it."

Logan fearfully asked, "And what if she catches us? Then what? There goes our souls."

Ethan, frowning as if he wanted to take Logan's soul himself, "Look, all we have to do is make a run to the car again and get out of here!"

Logan replied "Yeah? You do know that she knows where we live, right, Mr.-I-have-all-the-plans."

Ethan rolled his eyes. "Do you have any other ideas, Mr. Logan? Don't forget, I can leave your tail right here." So they both made a run for it.

Mrs. Johnson turned around as soon as she heard their footsteps through the leaves. Mrs. Johnson ran behind them, but Logan and Ethan successfully jumped back into the car. Mrs. Johnson ran right in front of the car, and Ethan stomped down on the gas pedal and they shot toward her. It struck, tossing her up in the air and she landed on her back. Ethan stopped the car and got out to see if she was still breathing while Logan yelled, "Ethan, get back in the damned car before she gets up and kills you!"

Ethan crept slowly towards Mrs. Johnson's still form. When he used his foot to nudge her, Mrs. Johnson turned over suddenly and reached for Ethan's legs. He jumped back and fell to the ground.

Logan moved over to the driver's seat and started to drive the car in reverse. While Ethan rolled over out of the way the car rolled over Mrs. Johnson again, shattering her against the concrete. As Ethan rolled onto his side he lay there for a while, exhausted.

Logan jumped out of the car to see if Ethan was Okay. "Hey man, are you Okay? Are you hurt?" Ethan just lay there, still on his side. Then he replied "Yeah," as he turned and looked sideways to Logan then over at Mrs. Johnson, "just promise me that after tonight you will not hit any more old people. Will you do that for me?"

Logan held his hand out to help Ethan up. He smiled as he pulled Ethan off the ground. "Yeah, I can do that. Come on let's go home."

However, Ethan looked down at Mrs. Johnson's body. "Well, what are we going to do with her?"

Logan also looked down at their former teacher. "I don't know. Leave her ass there."

Ethan turned back to Logan. "We just can't leave her here in the middle of the street. She was our English teacher, Logan."

Logan frowned, "She is not my damn English teacher. She is yours. And besides, I never liked her anyhow."

Ethan turned back and looked at Logan. "Look, you're going to help me move this body or I'm going to crown you one good time. Just try me, Mr. Matthew."

Logan looked around to find a place to dump the body. "Where the hell are you going to dump her body? We are out here in the middle of nowhere, Ethan."

Ethan started to look around, then started to think about how they buried Mr. Benjamin Jackson.

# Chapter 19

"Let's dump her body back into the cemetery like we did Old man Jackson."

Logan turned back at Ethan. "Are you sure this is going to work this time? And she won't get up from the grave?"

Ethan stared down at Mrs. Johnson, then back at Logan. "Yeah, I think this time it would work." Logan began to walk over to Mrs. Johnson's body. "Wait, I know you don't think that we are going to put her in this car... are we? No, Logan, please don't start that stuff again. We already have enough problems on our hands as it is." All Logan could do was shake his head.

"Okay then, tell me this Mr. Ethan, since you know every damn thing; what are we going to do about Ms. Cooper... in the freezer back at the school?" You know by now she is smelling up the place."

Ethan put his hands over his face as he kept on rubbing it. "Damn, I totally forgot about her. Now we have to go to the school tonight and move Ms. Cooper's body before someone else finds her."

Logan looked at Ethan. "Look man, I'm tired, hungry and sleepy, and I am ready to go home. These bodies are going to have to wait until the morning comes."

"What do you mean this has to wait until the morning? Like hell it will! You are going to help me bury this body just like you help me with Mr. Jackson. I told you Logan, if I have to go to the police and tell them everything we have done in the last two weeks I will. Don't try me Logan."

Logan rolled his eyes. "Okay, damn, are you going to help me move this body, cause her ass looks like she hasn't missed a meal in years."

Ethan walked back over to Logan and said in his soft voice, "You need to stop with all the jokes, Okay? This isn't the time to be doing a lot of laughing."

Logan regarded Ethan. "Who's joking? I'm dead serious. She looks like she hasn't missed a meal in years." Ethan sighed in irritation, "Will you just grab her legs while I get her arms?"

As Ethan went to bend down to pick up Mrs. Johnson, he raised his head back up to look at Logan. Waiting for Logan to move he called out, "Logan," Ethan used his brother's Logan's name with authority, "Look, I get it, you're tired. Well so am I, but we can not leave her in the middle of the road like this. Come on and quit playing, so we both can go home."

As the Matthew brothers bent down to move Mrs. Johnson Ethan happened to turn his head. He saw a black shadowy figure walking towards them. As Ethan tried to lift it became clear that it was a man in black denim overalls. Ethan pushed Logan over on to the ground. "Man, what the hell is wrong with you?" As Ethan started crawling his way backwards from Mr. Jackson, Logan finally caught sight of what Ethan was backing away from. Logan hurriedly got up off of the ground and both of the Matthew brothers ran back towards their car.

Mr. Jackson slowly walked towards the car, and when he put both of his hands on the trunk lid. The power slowly died out. Ethan kept trying to turn the engine over again and again, but all he was getting was a crank sound.

"Man, come on..." Logan yelled out to Ethan. Ethan turned his head as he was still trying to turn the ignition switch. "Come on, baby, please turn over for me." The more Ethan would turn the key the more Mr. Benjamin drained from the battery.

Logan looked back through the back window of the car, and he could see Mr. Jackson getting weak and turning blue. Logan hit Ethan on the arm. "Look man, he's getting weak, keep turning the key." Ethan couldn't believe his eyes. All he could do was keep on turning that ignition switch.

"Damn, why won't this thing turn over?" Logan turned and watched Mr. Benjamin Jackson falling to the ground. Logan went to open the door, but Ethan pulled Logan back in. "Hey man, don't get out of the car. You don't know if that thing is trying to play dead or not, and I'm not trying to lose my baby brother all over again."

Logan yelled in response. "You're right, I don't need that thing to get me again." The Matthew brothers stared one another pensively, while Ethan tried again to start the car one more time. All it did was make a cranking sound once again. Ethan leaned his head on to the steering wheel as he continued to turn the key.

"Please, dammit... start!" His voice had started to crack as if he was getting ready to cry. Ethan raised his head and looked toward Logan, "I don't think we are going to make it back home bro."

Logan returned a straight faced look. "Stop playing, Ethan, start the damn car."

Ethan looked at Logan solemnly. "It just won't start, Logan."

Logan started to turn from frustrated to scared, "Man, if you don't start this car, I swear on my life, I will just give you to Mr. Jackson. Now, start the damned car." Ethan turned the key once again, and the car began to start up. "Well, come on, let's get the hell out of here."

Ethan caught sight of Mrs. Johnson in the side view mirror. Wait. "We can't leave her in the middle of the road like that. We have to move her."

Logan turns Ethan incredulously. "Man, you get on my nerves. Why do we have to go back and get her? She just tried to kill both of us. Like I said, let's leave her tail right where she is."

Ethan looked back at Logan, "If we leave her there, they are going to know that we were the last people to see her alive."

Logan lean his head back, and looked sideways towards Ethan. "No, they not, trust me. It was a hit and run. All we have to say is the last time we saw her, was at school. We do not know anything... Okay? So stop being so scared about everything Okay? I got you." Logan turned back towards the window, and he began to smile as Ethan drove down the highway headed towards home.

After a long pause Ethan replied, "Yeah, Okay." After awhile of driving Ethan noticed a weird sound coming from the trunk. "Did you hear that noise?"

"Yeah, I hear it. Pull over and let's see what it is."

As the Matthew brothers steered to the side of the road Ethan asked in a panicky tone, "What if it's that thing again or what if..."

Logan hollered out, "Look man, whatever it is we are in this together, no matter what! Okay?! Besides, I'll admit, I did get us into this mess. So I'm going to get us out of this." Both brothers got out of the car and rushed to see what the noise could have been. Logan turns to Ethan, "Remember, we are in this together." When Logan opened up the trunk there lay Mr. Haywood inside. "What the hell are you doing in my trunk, you creep?"

Mr. Haywood went to climb out of the trunk, but Logan back-handed their old neighbor. "That's for kicking me in my side you old dirty bastard."

Ethan jumped in between Mr. Haywood and Logan. "Okay, Logan let's give him a chance to explain why he's trying to kill us."

Logan turned toward Ethan. "Explain? Explain what? How he's trying to kill us. Hell no, I'm not going to listen to somebody who just tried to kill me. Besides, we know that he was the one who dug up Mr. Jackson's body.

Mr. Haywood sat up, "Look, I know you boys don't trust me right now, but I'm telling you that ghost is trying to kill me, too."

Logan looked back and forth between his brother and Haywood. "You'd better not be lying, either, or so help me, I will kill you myself."

Haywood regarded both of the Matthew brothers, and took a deep breath. "Okay, no more funny stuff. If I try anything at all, you can kill me."

Logan leaned down to glare at Haywood. "Oh for sure that will happen. Don't tempt me, old man."

"Well, come on and get in the car. We can give you a lift ho..."

Logan cut Ethan off there, "The hell we will! His ass is going to walk. He is not getting in the same car with me."

Mr. Haywood pleaded with Logan, "Please, you have my word; no more funny stuff, Okay? I just want to know what happened to my twin brother and go home, that's all."

Logan walked back over toward where Haywood sat. "Yeah, yeah." He said as he pushed Mr. Haywood back into the trunk. Ethan briefly challenged Logan, "Why would you do that?"

Logan replied with, "You can go in there with him," in his low-tone voice.

Ethan shrugged and sighed, "Whatever, come on we have to get home so we can get these nasty, smelly clothes off of us." Ethan stopped as he pulled the car door open. And then look over at Logan . "Yeah, 'cause I smell you from way over here."

Logan snapped back at Ethan. "You know what you can do for me, right?" and he stuck his middle finger up in the air. Both of the Matthew brothers looked at one another and began to laugh.

Ethan turned and looked at Logan as they headed home. "You know, we haven't laughed like this in awhile. I do miss that bro."

Logan faced back at Ethan. "Don't you start trying to get all sentimental on me now. We still have a ghost to kill, and maybe a half human being." He looked back at the back seat of the car, as they pulled into the driveway. Then he got out of the car, opened the trunk and commanded Haywood, "Remember old man; no funny stuff. You got me?" with grim look on his face.

The Matthew brothers stood beside each other to watch Haywood walk away. Ethan asked Logan, "Do you think we can trust him?"

Logan turned to walk away and said back over his shoulder, "I just don't know, but if we can't we will just have to end up doing him just like we did Mrs. Johnson," and they both went silent entering the house.

Logan brought back up the tough question of, "What are we going to do about Ms. Cooper's dead body in the freezer?"

Ethan tiredly looked at Logan. "Dag man, I keep forgetting about her."

Logan stopped at the bottom of the stairs, exasperated, "Why do you keep saying that? You know damn well her body is in that freezer"

Ethan replied, "Don't start, please not now. I'm tired and I'm hungry..." He looked over at Logan pleadingly.

"Well, I think we need to get up a little early to move Ms. Cooper's body, don't you?" However the worn look on his face said that he could care less. "I mean, right about now I don't care who moves it, as long as they don't try to pin it on me.

"Look, it's already getting late. So let's talk about this in the morning, Okay?"

As the Matthew brothers got up for school Ethan reminded Logan, "We don't have that much time before the school opens up."

As they both got dressed for school Logan sought reassurances, "So, are you sure that Mr. Haywood is not going to try any more funny stuff?"

Ethan thought, then replied, "I think he gave us his word."

Logan halted in the middle of putting his clothes on and gave Ethan a long look. "That's your problem: you trust too many people – especially Mr. Haywood. You know damn well he is going to try something again. Watch and see if he don't."

Ethan looked back at Logan and just shook his head. "Well come on, we're going to be late for school, and I don't want to be late messing around with you."

Logan fired back at Ethan, "When have you ever been late? You always been on time thanks to me."

Ethan rolled his eyes. Sometimes you make me sick, you know that? Like I said, I don't want to be late and besides, we have to get Ms. Cooper out of the freezer."

Logan paused and looked at Ethan with a smile on his face. When he noticed Ethan returned his brother's gaze. "Logan, what are you smiling for, and what's so funny?"

As Logan walked out of the room to go downstairs, he halted long enough to reply, "Because you remember Ms. Cooper... that's why I'm smiling."

Ethan turned and gave Logan an evil look. "Okay Logan, don't start with me today I will make sure that Mr. Jackson takes your soul."

Logan shone with an even bigger smile. "You keep forgetting, brother, he already tried to take my soul, but he couldn't handle the spirit that he was tasting."

Ethan looked at Logan and then walked away.

As the Matthew brothers arrived at school. Ethan took charge, "We have to be careful so no one will see us."

But was readily deflated when Logan questioned, "And what part of the school are you talking about sneaking into without all of the teachers and the principal seeing you?"

Ethan recovered, "Watch and learn little brother..." Ethan walked over to a fire alarm, but Logan ran and jumped in front of him.

"Oh no you don't, we are not doing that again!"

Ethan gave Logan with an irritated look. "What the hell is wrong with you? We have to get that smelly dead body out of the cafeteria, or they are going to believe it was us that killed Ms. Cooper  Then they'll find out about Mr. Jackson, Mrs. Johnson,...

Logan stepped back, bending down as he began to laugh. "Will you stop being so uptight? My God, loosen up for crying out loud. You're really going to have everyone here looking at us. Besides, this is our last week in this dump, anyhow. So don't screw it up for me."

Ethan turned his head as if he had a demon in him. "What do you mean this is your last week in this dump? If you hadn't been acting crazy in the cemetery two weeks ago then I wouldn't be in this mess! I wouldn't be looking over my shoulder every five minutes."

Logan turned and looked at Ethan as he took a deep breath in, "Are you done yet? 'Cause we still have to move Ms. Cooper out of the freezer, you idiot. Look, you can do what you want. I'm going in here to see if I can move this dead body. Are you coming or not, it's up to you Ethan?"

Ethan started in the direction of the cafeteria. "You'd better not screw this up, either. So help me, I will kill you myself."

Logan stepped back from Ethan looking at him as if he lost his mind.

# Chapter 20

The Matthew brothers entered the cafeteria already noticing that the smell of Ms. Cooper had gone. Ethan put his hand out to the side to halt Logan. Did you smell that?"

Logan leaned his head back and sniffed giving Ethan a strange look. "Smell what? I don't smell anything. Come on, so we can get Ms. Cooper out of here before someone sees us."

Ethan stated haltingly, "Right... neither do I..." As they both walked over to the freezer to see if Ms. Cooper was still there the cafeteria lady Ms. Joyner came walking in.

"Oh snap, it's the head lunch lady!" said Logan pushing Ethan under a lunch table.

Ethan whispered harshly at Logan. "Really... this is the best you can do is to push me under a table? Where she can..." but by the time Ethan went to finish his sentence Logan had covered his mouth with a hand.

"What the hell is she doing here so early?"

"Well, she is the lunch lady... she has to be here early, Logan."

Logan shushed Ethan, "She's going to hear us."

Ms. Joyner came dancing into the cafeteria as if she had a hot date. Logan and Ethan shared a quizzical look. "Why is she coming in here singing like she had a man or something? Everyone knows that Ms. Joyner doesn't have a man. That's why she keeps on serving that nasty tuna fish and sour orange juice every week." Ethan's body shook as if he could still taste and smell that combination in his mouth.

Ms. Joyner walked over to the freezer. Logan looks over at Ethan imperatively. "We have to stop her from going into that freezer. What if Ms. Cooper's body scares the hell out of her and gave her a heart attack.

Ethan chimed in, "That would be a good idea, now wouldn't it – No more nasty ass tuna fish and sour orange juice."

Logan leaned his head back and looked at Ethan with a frown. "Will you stop joking the food? We have to get Ms. Cooper out of here before the witch lady sees her in there."

Ethan scowled back at Logan, "Oh, you can make jokes about the old witch, but I can't? I see where this is going."

Logan looked back at Ethan again. "Will you shut up before she hears and sees us?" However, Ms. Joyner kept right on dancing to the music that was playing only inside her head. "Damn, we are never going to get that body out of that freezer."

"Like hell we ain't," Ethan rolled out from under the table, "all we have to do is distract her, and then you can go and see if the body is still there."

Logan gave Ethan a weird look. "And how we are supposed to do that? Show her Ms. Cooper's dead body? 'Cause if we do that, I know she's going to run like hell."

Ethan laughed and Logan looked as if he wanted to punch him. "Will you cut it out? Can you be serious just for once? My god!" Logan rolled from under the table to sneak his way over towards the freezer.

He looked at Ethan while sticking his tongue out – all Ethan could do was shake his head. When Logan opened the freezer to remove Ms. Cooper he found that she was gone. Logan tried to looked towards Ethan, but by the time Logan shut the freezer Ms. Joyner was coming from the other side of the lunch room. She looked over at Logan shocked. "What are you doing here? It's not time for lunch yet, my dear." While she still sang the song from within her head Logan looked desperately at Ethan, but then offered, "Well, um... Mrs. Joyner, I came in here to see if you still had some of that delicious tuna fish." Ethan had looked a little green as if he wanted to throw up.

Logan hunched his shoulders. Ethan looked back at Logan and whispered, "Will you hurry the hell up?" As he tried gesturing to get Logan to open the freezer Ms. Joyner, who continued to talk.

Logan spoke to Mrs. Joyner loudly over his shoulder, "Okay, I see that you don't have anymore of that nasty ass... er, I mean good old tuna fish. So... I'll be heading back to class." Ethan looked at Logan incredulously. Ms. Joyner walked away – headed back into the kitchen as if she didn't hear a thing.

Logan ran back over to where Ethan had been crouched down. "What the hell was that all about?"

Logan frowned, "What are you talking about? I tried to get Ms. Cooper out, but she is not there."

Ethan gaped at Logan in disbelief. "What do you mean she is not there?"

"If I have to draw a picture for you... Do you smell her Ethan?"

"No"

"'Cause I don't... and I know damn well you don't either."

Ethan gasped in shock, "Do you think that Mr. Jackson came back for her?"

Logan looked at Ethan sideways. "Why the hell would he do that? She's already dead. What would he want with a dead body?"

Ethan started walking away, but stopped at the lunchroom door. "I don't know but something is not right here. Come on let's get back to class before the security guard sees us."

As the Matthew brothers head back to class. Ethan noticed that the halls had started to get a little chilly. Ethan asked Logan, "Do you feel that?

Logan stopped, too, "Ethan, why do you keep saying you're feeling and smelling things? I don't smell or feel anything. Come on, we can't be late for class, and this is my last week here in this dump – Thank you, Jesus!"

Ethan cocked his head at Logan, "Oh, now you want to call on him. Why didn't you call on him when Mr. Jackson was trying to kill us?"

Logan stepped back and rolled his eyes. "Whatever, I'm going to class."

Ethan halted and reminded Logan, "We still have to find Ms. Cooper's body, you do know that right?"

He waved Ethan off as he entered his classroom. Ethan sneered at Logan's back while walking into his own classroom. Entering, he noticed that there was a new math teacher: Mrs. Chance – the worst math teacher that anyone could have. Ethan thought to himself, 'Now what the hell would Mr. Harrison get Mrs. Chance for? I can't stand this lady, nor can I stand the way she teaches. Think Ethan, think! How can I get out of this classroom?'

The more Ethan tried to think, the more Mrs. Chance would talk with that squeaky voice. 'Oh My God! Do I really have to listen to her and that damned voice today.'

Mrs. Chance looked over where Ethan was seated. "Mr. Matthew do we have a problem, sir?"

Ethan slid down into the chair with his hand over his face, then looked up and answered, "No ma'am, I just have a terrible headache. May I be excused for today"

Mrs. Chance looked at Ethan, "Well, child you just got here... Yes, you can go to the nurse's office."

When he got out to the hall, Ethan pulled out his cellphone and called his brother. Logan looked down when his phone rang, and he hit ignore. So Ethan traveled straight from his classroom to Logan's. He looked in through door window. Logan looked up and saw Ethan standing there waving his hands and mouthing, 'Will you come here, dammit?' Logan frowned, wondering why the hell was Ethan standing there, so he got up and ran to the door. "What's wrong with you? Is Mr. Jackson after you again?"

Ethan gave Logan with a strange look. "No! I had to get out of my math class because of Mrs. Chance's voice. I couldn't take any more of her squeaky voice."

Logan stepped back and looked at Ethan as if he were crazy. "What the hell do you mean you couldn't take anymore of her voice? I thought that crazy ghost had came after you or something, and you're telling me that you just can't take any more of your math teacher's voice. What the hell, Ethan? are you insane or you have just lost your damn mind?"

Ethan leaned his head to one side. "No, I haven't lost my mind. I just don't want to hear that squeaky annoying sound.

Logan glared at Ethan, and in a soft low voice, "Get away from me, now." Ethan hung his head and walked away.

# Chapter 21

Later that afternoon Mr. B. Harrison came around to each classroom asking all of the teacher's if they had seen Ms. Cooper. However, none of them had seen her since the previous week. Mr. Harrison had stopped in the middle of the hallway to think, 'I wonder if the children have seen Ms. Cooper anytime this week. I'll bet those Matthew brothers saw her. They always seem to know what goes on around this school, no matter if there is trouble or not. They are surely going to know.' As Mr. Harrison began to walk back down the hallway it turned out that Ethan was coming toward him, and Mr. Harrison looked up at the right time to see him. "What are you doing out of class, young man, and why don't you have any of your books in your hands my son?" Ethan at Mr. Harrison and smiled. "What is supposed to be so funny, Mr.

Matthew? I should put you in detention since you don't have any of your books with you, or a hall pass."

Ethan stepped back away from Mr. Harrison as his smile left his face. "Well sir, I was on my way to the nurse's office because..." and when he paused Mr. Harrison caught his straight, serious look.

Mr. Harrison didn't let him finish when he moved on to, "Well, since you are out in the hallway, you can tell me if you saw Ms. Cooper this week."

Ethan's eyes widened as he started to step back away from Mr. B. Harrison. "Ah... no, sir, I haven't seen her at all because... I think she is ... ah, sick. Why don't you call her house to see if she is Okay." Mr. Harrison looked at Ethan with confusion across his face at first, but the look of wanting to throw him into in-school-suspension for the rest of the day returned. "Well, Mr. Harrison, I have to get back to class. It was nice talking to you, have a good day, Mr. Harrison... sir." Ethan turned around and started to walk as fast as his legs could take him. Ethan ran back to Logan's classroom and looked back in through the window. Ethan waved his hand at Logan again. The latter looked over and waved Ethan off with a frown, telling Ethan to go away.

Ethan, however, persisted in waving at Logan to come to him, so Logan decided to come and see what his pest of a brother wanted. "What is your problem? You are going to get me into trouble and, so help me if I get into trouble, I am going to make sure that Ms. Joyner and Mr. Jackson get your tail. Now what is it?"

Ethan looked sternly at Logan. "Look man, Principal Harrison is looking for Ms. Cooper."

Logan looked at Ethan as if he was lying. "What... what do you mean that Mr. Harrison is looking for Ms. Cooper?"

Ethan added imperative to his tone. "Just like I said, he is looking for her, and if we don't find her body we are going to be in big trouble."

Logan turned and looked back at Ethan. "What do you mean that 'we are going to be in trouble'? First of all, I didn't have anything to do with this dead body. Don't come and try to threaten me about Ms. Cooper. I can care less about her, now."

Ethan, at first taken aback, then feigning nonchalance said, "Okay then I just see you in jail." Ethan added a chuckle as he turned to walk away. "Oh yeah, and by the way, what size underclothes you wear?"

Logan made a face at his back, then he returned to his classroom. As Ethan began to walk away he felt a cool breeze up against his face. This made him stop in the middle of the hallway and rub his face. 'I know this can't be Mr. Jackson again. Lord please not right now. I have to find Ms. Cooper, and I have two more weeks before I graduate.' Ethan kept on walking, but the more he walked, the more he could feel the coldness on his face. "Okay Mr. Jackson, I know you are here so let's cut to the chase." And so Mr. Benjamin Jackson's hollow body started to appear from the cold air. Ethan's eyes widened. As Mr. Jackson slowly walked toward Ethan and wrapped his cold, hollow hand around Ethan's throat.

Ethan struggled to get Mr. Jackson's cold hand from around his neck, but the more Ethan would fight the tighter Mr. Jackson's grip seemed. Then the ghastly form lifted Ethan off the floor and opened Ethan's mouth to suck the life out of him. Suddenly, at the time he started that, Mr. Harrison came around the corner. He looked up at Ethan dangling from the hollow shadow being, but fear had struck his whole body. All he could do was stand there frozen, as if he was a block of ice – even when Mr. Benjamin Jackson turned his hollow shadow body around and began to reach for Mr. Harrison. The ghost slowly put Ethan down on the floor while walking towards the principal. Mr. Harrison finally looked around and saw the fire alarm and pulled it.

The noise sounded off and everyone came out of their classroom. Mr. Jackson's ghost howled at Mr. Harrison, then turned and looked back at Ethan. "This is not over," in his ghost voice, "I will get your soul – I want my revenge." Then he disappeared. Mr. B. Harrison ran over to Ethan and tried to help him off the floor. As the students poured out of their classrooms Ethan and Mr. Harrison were left looking for the ghostly form, then at one another. Ethan looked gravely when he said, "You can't tell no one what you saw or they are going to think you are crazy," just as Mr. Harrison was trying to figure out if they had been hallucinating or if he was straight losing his mind.

"What? What do you mean we can't tell anyone? Have you lost your mind kid? That thing, or … whatever it was, just try to kill me… tried to kill you! Then, you tell me that I can't tell anybody?!"

Since Mr. Harrison started to get loud Ethan pulled him closer, "What the hell is wrong with you old man? I just specifically told you that you can not tell anybody, man. What the hell is wrong with you old people?"

Mr. Harrison, flustered, let out a big breath of air.

When he saw Ethan and Mr. Harrison standing In the middle of the hallway Logan began to walk toward them. "Hey bro, why are you still standing in the hallway after I told you to go to class?" When he drew closer he looked back and forth between the two of them and asked, "Okay can you tell me why our principal is standing out here like he just saw a ghost?"

Ethan held his head sideways while looking at Logan with a frown on his face. Logan stepped back and looked at both of them. "Come on, man. I just know damn well that he didn't see Mr. Jackson. Ethan, please tell me he didn't.

Ethan looked him up and down and walked away. "We have to make sure that he doesn't say anything to anyone or we are doomed."

Logan followed, "What do you mean 'we'? We didn't have anything to do with it because I wasn't here!"

Ethan looked at Logan coolly. "You keep right on saying that. Well, don't you forget all about Mr. Benjamin Jackson, Okay? You were there for that one." When Logan started to say something else Ethan cut him off, "Look, we just have to make sure that he doesn't say anything about Mr. Jackson, Okay?"

As Logan looked at Mr. Harrison, then back at Ethan. "Wait a minute, I thought you had the name tag, Ethan. Why didn't you use the name tag on him?"

Ethan put his hand on his forehead. "Aww man, I totally forgot I had his name tag in my pocket." Ethan reached his hand in his left pocket and pulled Mr. Jackson's name tag out.

Mr. Harrison looked over Ethan's shoulder and asked, "What is that."

Logan turned towards Mr. Harrison. "Something that would have killed the unwanted ghost, if only someone would have used it."

Ethan looked from Logan, with a frown to principal Harrison at whom he beamed a smile. "Are you going back to your office, sir, and doing some paperwork, or something?"

# Chapter 22

Logan declared to Ethan, "I'm telling you now, if he goes to tell someone we have to get rid of him. He is going to be a big problem." Ethan turned his head to watch the departing principal.

"So what do you want to do with him Logan – kill him?"

Logan replied coldly, "That's your best bet. That's the only chance we got, because if we go down he damn sure has to go down, and I'm not talking about going to jail either. I want to graduate next week, and I know for damn sure you want to, too. So are you down, or what?" Ethan gave him a stunned look, but then sighed, "Yeah, I'll do it, but only one condition. You have to help me find Ms. Cooper and make sure that Mr. Haywood doesn't go to the police."

Logan replied in kind, "You don't have to worry about Mr. Haywood. I'm going to take care of him myself."

Mr. Harrison, still walking away down the corridor, turned back to see the boys and Ethan put his one finger over his lips as a reminder. The principal continued walking down the hallway. "I don't think he is going to tell anyone. Besides, after what he saw, I think he's a little shook up."

Logan turned to face Ethan. "You'd better hope so or, like I said, he will join the others, and that's a promise."

Ethan reminded, "Well, it's time to go to lunch and taste some of that..."

Logan cut him off with a look. "Ethan, you better not say it or, so help me, you will be eating that nasty tuna." Soon as Logan said that word Ethan's whole body shook. Logan regarded Ethan and started to laugh, "Hey, bro you want some sour orange juice?"

Ethan turned and rolled his eyes. "That's not funny, Logan." Ethan walked away. "Hey, don't be mad bro, you know you like that sour orange juice and nasty tuna fish." Logan kept on laughing while he walked behind Ethan as they both entered the lunchroom. As they both entered the lunch line they noticed that Ms. Joyner wasn't serving tuna. "Hey man, what's for lunch today? I don't see any of that nasty ass tuna. Do you think she ate some and decided not to serve it today?" Logan turned back to Ethan with a big smile on his face. "I don't know... that's your tuna and sour orange juice."

As Logan burst out in another loud laugh he started to bend over. Ethan rolled his eyes. "You always think everything is a joke, don't you?"

Logan continued to laugh, "Come on man, you know you want to laugh, too."

Ethan pause, then began to laugh, too. "I guess you're right it is funny, now that you mention it."

Logan straightened up "Hey, you don't think that Ms. Joyner is serving Ms. Cooper do you. You know she was in the freezer."

Ethan looked down at his food and immediately started to gag. "Why the hell would you say that? Now I don't want anything to eat."

Logan harped back on, "Good 'cause we still have to make sure that Mr. Harrison doesn't say anything to anyone."

Ethan still studied his food, then looked back up at Logan. "What about Ms. Cooper? What if this is her that we are about to eat?"

Logan took on a serious look. "What the hell is wrong with you? I was just joking, my god! Get a grip man, loosen up before you have a heart attack. Look, we still have to make sure that Mr. Haywood and Mr. Harrison don't go to the police."

Ethan replied, getting tired of it all. You already said that to me, I get it. We have to make sure that both of them don't go to the police, and so on and so on. Okay I get it. What's next? Now, what do we do with this food that we aren't going to eat?

Logan just held his head down and took in a big breath and let it out. He began to rub his forehead. "Throw it in the trash Ethan, I really don't care what you do with it." As both of the Matthew brothers kept on going back and forth, Mr. Harrison strode into the cafeteria, Logan stopped and just stared. "I think he is going to tell the other teachers what happened in the hallway, Ethan."

Ethan intently watched, as well. "Logan, I don't think he is going to tell them anything. Besides, he knows if he tells he might just be next."

Mr. Harrison searched for and found the Matthew brothers while he continued to pour his coffee. He walked over and sat down at the table. "Look, I'm not going to tell anyone what I saw today, but you have to tell me who or what was that thing that had you up in the air."

Ethan looked at Logan and then back at the principal. "What are you talking about, Mr. Harrison. I didn't see anything that had me up in the air. I think you are drinking too much of that coffee."

Mr. Harrison took his cup down away from his lips and looked at Ethan with a strange look. "When I was coming around the corner... that thing had you in the air... you were off of your feet young man. Don't sit here and make it seem like I'm the crazy one." Ethan's act included staring at Mr. Harrison as if he had lost his mind. He, in turn, looked at both of the boys and then started to grin. "I know what you are trying to do here, but it won't work, I know what I saw, and I'm going to make sure that the news people know about it."

Logan turned and looked at Ethan with one eyebrow raised. "I told you he was going to tell someone. Now he definitely has to go."

Ethan still tried to get a handle on Mr. B. Harrison, "Sir, you really got to stop drinking that caffeine, man. It's starting to make you see things that's not there."

Mr. Harrison got up from the table eyes flicking back and forth between the Matthew brothers. "This is not over. I am going to prove what I saw, and when I do, I'm going to make sure that you two boys are held accountable for this mess."

Logan slowly at Ethan with I-told-you-so in his eyes. "Oh, I'm going to kill him now."

Ethan grabbed Logan by the arm. "Wait! No one is going to believe him anyhow. Everyone in the school thinks he is crazy, so this is our chance to get rid of him for good," Logan looked at Ethan with his finger pointing at him, but before Logan could say anything Ethan had cut him off, "...and without killing anyone, Logan." All Logan could do was frown and walk away.

# Chapter 23

By that afternoon the Matthew brothers had decided to keep a close eye on Mr. B. Harrison.  Ethan reminded Logan, "Okay well, we have to get back to class.  Remember, Logan, we cannot kill Mr. Harrison."

Logan rolled his eyes at Ethan as he walked away.  Then he stopped in the middle of the hallway to look back at Ethan.  "You know he is going to tell... no matter what you say.  All he needs to do is go to the news and, boom, the story is out all about the Matthew brothers seeing ghosts.  Is that what you want to happen Mr. Ethan?"

Ethan lowered his head.  "I don't know what to do anymore, Logan.  All I want is this thing to stop following me, and for us to get our lives back.  That's all I want."

Logan too steps back toward Ethan. "Well I suggest that you let me go ahead and do what I have to do, which is to kill him so we won't have this problem."

"Logan, how are we going to seduce him to where we are?"

Logan leaned his head back and looked at Ethan with a weird look. "What do you mean seduce him? We not having sex with the man, Ethan"

"All we're going to do is try and convince him that he didn't see what he thought had seen," clarified Ethan, frowning, I could have sworn that I said that about two hours ago in the lunchroom. You dingbat, It's no different than what I was just trying to do."

"Okay then, we kill him, plain and simple. You have any other ideas in mind, Mr. Ethan?"

Ethan took a deep breath in "No, I don't, but I do know that I don't want to kill him."

Logan turned on Ethan with low and gravelly frustration. "Okay, suit yourself, but when he goes to the police don't say I didn't tell you so."

Ethan glared back at Logan. "Okay, so what if we do kill him? What is that going to solve? He is going around asking questions about Ms. Cooper, the math teacher we haven't found yet, Mr.-I-want-to-kill-everyone.

Logan closed in on Ethan, and snorting in rage, "Right about now I want to kill you! Don't push me Ethan, cause you will end up next. Mom and dad will have one less son to think about, then in his soft voice he continued, "Keep trying me."

Ethan rolled his eyes. "Whatever, I'm going back to class and you need to go also."

Logan turned, unable to drop the debate, "If someone wouldn't come to my class with all this mess they keep creating."

By the time Ethan wanted to say something more Logan had cut him off. "I... I ... whatever. I'm going to class. I'll see you later."

*Linda Spence Howard*

As both of the Matthew brothers entered their classed. Mr. B. Harrison was standing in one of the classroom doorways listening. 'I knew those boys were up to no good... now is my chance to expose them without them trying to kill me.'

Later on that afternoon, as the school let out, the Matthew brothers met up with one another. Ethan looked at Logan, "...and remember; we can't do any more killing, Okay?"

Logan presented Ethan with a look that said he cared less. "Yeah, I heard you. No more killing. Hey, do you know what you're going to wear for graduation? As they walked out of the building Mr. Harrison stopped them at the doorway.

"Don't think I don't know what two boys have been up to. I am going to make sure that the police and the school board find out about you."

Ethan and Logan first looked at one another then at Mr. Harrison, "I have no idea what you are talking about. What is wrong?"

Before Ethan could get the rest of the words out of his mouth the principal cut him off. "Look here kid, don't try and act like you don't know what I'm talking about. I overheard you talking about how you killed Ms. Cooper." Ethan turned and looked over at Logan. All Logan offered was a raised eyebrow.

After long seconds of meeting Principal Harrison's gaze, Logan replied, "Sir, I think you got us boys mixed up with someone us..."

Mr.Harrison shot back, cutting him off, "Don't try me kid, I'm already hip to the games that you young kids nowadays are doing," as he pointed his finger into Logan's face.

Logan looked coolly past the finger at Mr. Harrison, then he took his hand and slowly and pushed the finger out of his face.

"Like I said, I don't know what you're talking about. So I suggest you let my brother and I go on."

Mr. B. Harrison was still standing close to Logan's face when he quietly replied, "Okay, then, I'm going to let you and your freak brother go."

Logan, sensing victory puffed up before Mr. Harrison, "Who the..." but Ethan had stepped in between them.

"Okay Logan, let's go, you know how mom and dad want us home on time." Ethan began to push Logan backward as the latter still cast lethal eyes at Mr. Harrison. As both of the Matthew brothers got into the car Logan turned to Ethan. "I know damn well he didn't just accuse us of something that we didn't do! He got to go, Ethan! So help me, I will kill the old bastard myself!"

Ethan, still trying, "Will you calm down? He doesn't have any proof that we killed anyone. I've told you before they are trying to get rid of him, anyhow. So calm down, and let's just make sure that Mr. Haywood doesn't go to the police. That's the one that we need to be worried about."

Logan asked, but more like he was stating counterpoint, "And you're saying that we shouldn't be worried about Principle Harrison? He's the main one we need to be worried about. I told you what I was going to do to him if he gets in my way."

Ethan drove down the highway. "No more killing, Logan, you promised me."

Logan looked at Ethan with a frown. "I didn't promise you anything. And besides, I told you if he gets in our way that he has to go. Now he is in our way, so he got to go, plain and simple."

Ethan looked over Logan with his out thoughtfully. "You just a stone cold killer, you know that?

Logan smiled as he looked back at Ethan. "Thank you bro, For those kind words, I appreciate it." Then he looked out of the window and the rolling countryside for a long moment before adding, "but I still want to kill him."

Ethan frowned, "Will you let it go... please! He is not a threat, trust me. If you would have seen his face in the hallway, you wouldn't be too worried about him right now," he said in a soft tone.

Logan said strictly informatively, "That's my problem. I am worried."

# Chapter 24

As they pulled up to the house Mr. Haywood was standing on their front porch. The brothers got out of the car and went right up to the old man. "What are you doing here? What is it you want? We told you everything, so why are you here?"

Haywood stepped off of the porch and started to close the distance between them. "We have some unfinished business." Haywood reached into his coat pocket and pulled out a gun. Logan and Ethan started back away.

Logan's eyes darted at Ethan then at Haywood. "So you want to kill us... for killing your brother right?"

Haywood laughed. "As crazy as that sounds, but yes I'm going to kill you."

As he raised the gun to shoot, Logan and Ethan made a run for it. As the brothers ran into the house and slammed the door

*Linda Spence Howard*

Ethan pleaded, "Please, don't say I told you so. Wait until we kill this old bastard." Logan just shook his head. "Right now we don't have time to be pointing fingers at one another."

Logan nodded over his shoulder for Ethan to look across the room, "Let's run down to the basement. You know he doesn't like it there."

As they began to make a run for the basement Ethan sincerely looked back at Logan. "Hey man, I love you, Okay?"

Logan had stopped running to reply, "What the hell did I tell you about all that sentimental mess. Don't start Ethan – not now." As they entered the basement, Ethan started to look around for someplace to hide.

Haywood began to yell out, "I know where all of your hiding places are, so you might as well come out."

Ethan turned and looked over at Logan as they hid behind a stack of boxes. "Now what are we going to do?

Logan put one finger to his lips. "Shh, he can hear us." Logan looked around the basement for something with which to hit Haywood. "Damn, this would be a good time to have that golden candlestick."

Ethan raised his head up and looked around to see if he saw anything. He noticed an old, rusty iron pipe laying on the floor, but it was not close to them. Ethan nudged Logan and whispered, "Hey Logan, see if you can get that iron pipe. If he gets down here we can hit him with that."

All Logan did was smile with something akin to pride when he looked back at Ethan. He went over to the iron rusty pipe. "Now you talking bro." As Logan bent to grab the iron pipe the doorknob began to move. Logan ran back to hide back behind the boxes.

Haywood crept into the basement slowly. Logan put his finger on his lips. "Don't say anything," he whispered, "I want him to get a little closer so I can hit him." All Ethan could do was nod his head. Haywood moved all around the basement slowly. In a burst of motion Logan lept from behind the boxes and hit the older man over the head, but this time Mr. Haywood didn't fall.

Instead he turned around and looked right at Logan with a smile. "You thought you could knock me out with a pipe like you did before, huh, kid?"

Logan dropped the iron pipe and started to back up. His eyes widened as he couldn't believe what he had just seen or heard. Haywood went to reach for Logan, but Ethan emerged and picked up the iron pipe and swung it at Mr. Haywood once more. It connected, but Haywood had started to turn visibly into Mr. Benjamin Jackson and the basement air ran cold and smokey. Instead of crumpling to the floor Haywood's whole body seemed to twirl all around the basement. Logan and Ethan used that moment to try to make a run for it.

By the time they made it to the door Mr. Jackson had appeared and looked after Logan and Ethan. "Now that I have your attention, I want my revenge, I want your soul!"
They tried to look back at what they had thought was Haywood. It was made difficult because more and more of the heavy, gray, smoky winds filled the space. Logan and Ethan had started to cover their faces. Logan yelled, "I think we can make a run for it! Just stay close behind me!" However, when the Matthew brothers got close to the basement door Mr. Jackson swirled his way in front of it.

He looked gazed down at Logan and Ethan with blood red eyes. Mr. Jackson appeared part corporeal and half ghost. The brothers backed up. They wore terrified looks on their faces, as if they knew their souls were going to be taken.

Ethan cried out, "Now what are we going to do? He has the door blocked, and he is too strong to get past."

Logan kept on looking around to find a way out, but there was no use. The gray heavy clouds were too thick to see past.

Mr. Jackson's spirit started to appear as a whole man, and the gray, thick clouds had started to clear. Mr. Jackson's body slid down the wall and he stepped toward where Ethan and Logan were. The basement continued to get colder, and at the same time, Mr. Jackson began to slower. Logan and Ethan kept backing up, but then they kept tripping over the brown boxes. Ethan suddenly remembered that he had Mr. Jackson's name tag in his pocket.

He pulled out the name tag and held it up in the air. Logan looks over at Ethan. "Now you want to pull out the damn name tag... when he is two inch from us? You damned idiot!"

Ethan turned and looked back at Logan, "What was I supposed to do? I thought he was Mr. Haywood."

Logan turned and looked at Ethan with a frown. "Does that look like damned Mr. Haywood to you?"

As Ethan and Logan shot words back and forth at each other Mr. Benjamin Jackson let out a loud scream. Both of the Matthew brothers had to cover their ears.

Logan turned to Ethan while still covering his ears. "Ethan, point the name tag at him!" Ethan looks down at his hand then pointed the name tag directly at Mr. Jackson. Nothing happened. Actually, the longer Ethan pointed the name tag at Mr. Jackson the stronger it seemed he became.

Ethan turned away to look back at Logan, "It's not working! Now what?" Now he was steadily holding the name tag against Mr. Jackson's half human form. Ethan fell to his knees. "I can't hold my arm up no longer, Logan! He is too strong." Logan bent down to try to hold Ethan's arm up in the air. But Mr. Benjamin Jackson kept right on pushing through.

The walls inside of the basement begin to turn red and hot. Ethan and Logan still held up the name tag of Mr. Benjamin

Jackson. The floor of the basement had started to melt into a silvery liquid lava. They looked down at the floor, then back up at Mr. Jackson. The understanding that there was no way out of that basement was dawning upon them.

Logan came up with a new idea: "What if you toss the name tag at him? It might just kill him that way!"

All peered back at Logan, then at his hand. The longer he had held the name tag at Mr. Jackson, the closer he had gotten. Logan yelled to him, "Toss the name tag now!" Ethan threw his hand back and gave a big toss right into Mr. Benjamin Jackson's stomach. When the name tag touched Mr. Jackson's body a sudden, loud squealing sound rang out. Mr. Jackson violently swirled all around the basement again, and Ethan and Logan could hear him say, "I want my revenge, I want your soul!"

The more his ghost swirled around the room the more the body of Benjamin Jackson decomposed. The boys picked themselves up off the floor as they watched Mr. Jackson melting into the silver lava.

Logan looked over at Ethan indicating the floor with both hands, "Now, who in the hell is going to clean up this mess?"

Ethan replied with a big smile on his face. "Don't look at me. I already told you: I don't have anything to do with this." Ethan walked toward the basement door, then turned back at Logan, "hey bro, have some fun cleaning up." Ethan bent down to pick up the name tag, whirled around and tossed it at Logan. Logan caught Mr. Benjamin Jackson's name tag. "Ha ha ha, very funny, Ethan. What you need to be doing is helping me get your friend up." All Ethan did was laugh and walk away.

# Chapter 25

The next day, the Matthew brothers got up and got ready for school. Ethan turned to Logan, "Now we can finally get some rest, we don't have to worry about that ghost or his "so called" brother Mr. Haywood."

Logan replied, "Yeah, but we do have to worry about Principal Harrison; the one who said he is going to the police."

Ethan groaned, "Damn, I forgot all about him. How are we going to stop him?" Logan turned around with a big smile on his face. Ethan knew right then and there that he was going to have to clean up more of Logan's messes. "Don't you start that mess Logan. We have enough crap to worry about like graduation and applying for colleges." Logan leaned back and regarded Ethan with a strange look. "Oh, all of sudden you want to think about graduation. You better be worrying about the police, and hoping that they don't find

Mr. Haywood's body, or Mr.Jackson's." He looked Ethan up and down and added, "Ethan, you are a joke." All Ethan could do was frown and walk away.

When they arrived at school Mr. B. Harrison was standing in the doorway waiting for the Matthew brothers to walk in. "Hello boys, how did you sleep last night?"

As Logan was about to open his mouth Ethan cut him off. "It was fine Mr. Harrison, how did you sleep last night? Did you sleep with one eye open because you thought you were seeing ghosts?" Then Ethan looked back as he passed Mr. Harrison and began to laugh. Ethan and Logan continued to walk on, he then slyly smiled over at Logan.

Mr. Harrison stood there and rolled his eyes. You boys think you got away with this but, I promise you," as the Matthew brothers continued to walk on, Mr. Harrison got louder, "I will let the school board know what you did." The entire school stopped and turned around to look back at Principal Harrison. Then he began to look around and realized he was becoming a spectacle. However he pressed on, "This is not over. You will pay for what you have done." Then Mr. Harrison put one finger on his lip and tapped it over and over again. As he watched the Matthew brothers walk down the hallway. Assistant principal. Mrs. Megg Brown came down the hallway to him.

"May I ask you a couple of questions Mr. Harrison?" Mr. Harrison lowered his finger from his lip. He showed Mrs. Brown a frown that said he could care less about what she had to say.

"Yes, what is it?" He asked impatiently, "What could you possibly want now?" Mrs. Brown stepped back and looked over her glasses at Mr. Harrison. "I have heard that you're going around the school harassing the Matthew brothers. Please tell me that this isn't true."

Mr. Harrison was taken aback and gave her a weird look. "So what? What if I have been? What's it to you? Those boys have been getting into trouble ever since they got here, and I'm going to put a stop to it."

Mrs. Megg Brown leaned her head back a little further. "Sir, you are acting crazy, if someone found this all out, you might get put away."

Mr. Harrison laughed. "You're just mad because I know what goes on around this school before you do."

Mrs. Brown gave him a shocked look at that. She put one eyebrow up and grinned. "Like I said, you are crazy and you will be put away." She started to walk away, but stopped in the middle of the hallway and turned around. "The next time you threaten those boys you will be sorry," she added with a grave look on her face.

Later on that day, Logan and Ethan met up at the lunchroom. "Okay bro, I think we need to watch out for Mr. Harrison. He really is trying to get the both of us expelled before we graduate."

Logan wearily looked back at Ethan, "Not if I have anything to do with it. Oh, we will be graduating if I have to get rid of him myself."

Ethan's eyes widened up like the four of July firework. "Are you crazy? You can't kill him, Logan, they're going to know that we did it."

Logan leaned his head back exasperated. "Well, do you have any other suggestions?"

Ethan took a deep breath and shrugged at Logan.

"I didn't think so. Now we're going to do it my way." Ethan went to say something but Logan cut him off. "Your way only you got that." Ethan only nodded his head twice.

"Well come on so we can get…"

Now Ethan cut him off and turned around and faced Logan. "I wish the hell you would say it just one more time!"

All Logan could do was laugh as he walked a little closer to Ethan and put a hand on his shoulder. "All I was going to say was let's go eat," with a big smile on his face, knowing what Ethan was thinking. As Ethan and Logan went to stand in the lunchroom line Mr. Harrison had strode into the cafeteria. "Well, well, well boys, I see you have made it to the lunchroom after all. What will you be having for lunch this afternoon? Dead humans?" With a smile on his face.

"What the hell you mean by that, you dingbat?" Logan started to stand up to the principal, but Ethan stepped in and grabbed Logan by his arm.

"Look, Principal Harrison, my brother and I don't know what you are talking about. So please can you just leave us alone?" All Mr. B. Harrison did was glare at the Matthew brothers and keep on grinning.

"And for the record It's Principal Mister. B. Harrison to you."

Logan faced Ethan as he whispered under his breath, "It's more like jackass Principal B. Harrison." Ethan put his hand over his mouth to stifle a laugh.

Mr. Harrison stepped back and scowled. "And what, may I ask is so funny, Mr. Ethan?"

Ethan leaned his head back to look up at Mr. Harrison.

Logan cleared his throat to retort with, "I believe it's Mr. Matthew, sir. Mr. Harrison's only reply was to roll his eyes, and walk away. He was soon heading back down the hallways.

A few turned corners later, and he started to feel a cool breeze. He reared around to see where the cool breeze was coming from. Then he noticed the hallway was getting a little cloudy.

"Man, this school really needs to be fixed and up to date." With that he kept on walking down the hallway. The further he walked, the colder it got. He stopped once again and pulled up his shirt collar. He then turned back around, and there was Benjamin Jackson standing there in his blue denim overall jumpsuit. Mr. Harrison was at first dumbstruck and agape, then he tried to make a run for it. Mr. Jackson grabbed Mr. Harrison by his collar handily and hoisted him up into the air. When he tried to yell out for help no sounds came. Mr. Jackson's half-human hands slowly wrapped them around his neck.

He began to suck the breath right out of Principal Harrison. The more he drew out Mr. Harrison's life-breath the more human he became. It appeared as if Mr. Harrison was turning old and wrinkled, with blue, pale skin. With no one around the ghost kept right on sucking the life out of Mr. Harrison uninterrupted.

When he had finished Mr. B. Harrison off, he looked down at what was left of him. "Well, now you can't do me anymore good, now can you?" He turned and looked back down the hallway, and he said in his shadow voice, "I will get your soul, I will get my revenge." Then he swirled through the hallways leaving a black dusty, cloudy smoke behind.

# Chapter 26

As Logan and Ethan were leaving the lunchroom they noticed there was no sign of the principal. Ethan looked around, then mused, "I wonder where Mr. Harrison is. He normally sits in the hallway harassing students. I guess he has had a change of heart today."

Logan looked around and got the feeling of the place, then whispered, "No, something is not right about this hallway. You don't feel any cool breeze on your arms?"

Ethan at first rolled his eyes roll his eyes, but then laughed, "Please! Don't start that again. I just want to go on about my business, and leave it at that. Can you do that Logan just for once, please?!"

Logan replied, "Yeah, I can do that, but I'm telling you that something isn't right about this hallway. I can feel it, Ethan."

Ethan leaned his head over a little in Logan's direction. "You always feeling something, you know that? Now come on, I don't want to be late messing around with you again."

Logan stopped, cocked his head and replied to Ethan, "You know, I'm getting very tired of you telling me that."

Ethan glared back back. "Well, It's true. You do make me late for class."

Logan simply rolled his eyes and continued to walk down the hallway. As both of the Matthew brothers went their separate ways Assistant Principal Brown was coming down the hallway as fast as she could.

"Oh, boys wait, I wanted to know have you seen your principal?" She looked at the Matthew brothers with an unpleasant expression, and she began to huff and puff. Logan and Ethan turned around to answer Mrs. Brown. "No, we haven't," Logan turned his head away to whipster, "and don't want to either." Ethan gave Logan a look that said he wanted to smack him one good time.

Mrs. Megg Brown turned and looked over at Logan with a big smile on her face. "That's Okay boys I feel the same way about him, too." She turned her head and looked away as a chill came over her. She shook briefly. "Well, if you see him, please tell him that we have to sign off on the graduation diplomas."

Logan and Ethan looked at one another meaningfully. "Yeah, sure, if we see the old dingbat. Mrs. Brown then smiled and walked away. Logan remained looking at Ethan. "Man, I can't wait until next week comes. I'm going to tell all of those teachers, especially Mr. Harrison where to go."

Ethan leaned his head to one side. "I think you might want to hold off on the attitude. You haven't gotten the diploma yet, Mr. Logan."

He rolled his eyes in response to Ethan and said, "Well, when I do, they all will know exactly where the…"

Ethan stopped him with a yell of, "Logan! What's has gotten into you?" Logan's only reply was to turn his back and laugh.

Later that afternoon, Assistant Principal Brown had decided that all seniors could leave class early, so they could be fitted for their caps and gowns. She began to look all around for the principal again, and her face had begun to turn red. 'Where in the heck is that Mr. Harrison. He was supposed to be here an hour ago.' she mused. She began to calling out his name on her rounds in the halls. She started putting out calls for him on the loudspeaker, but still no answer, no arrival.

When the Matthew brothers arrived at the fitting Logan asked in front of Mrs. Brown, "Okay, now do you us believe me about the hallway?"

Ethan took in a deep breath. "Oh, well… at least we don't have to hear his mouth any more for today."

Logan leaned his head over to say quietly, "Are you crazy or was something in that lunch back there that we just ate? Has gotten into you that has you acting like me?"

Ethan sharply replied to Logan, "Hell No! I wouldn't dare act like you, not if they offered me a million dollars. Wait, yes I would, raking in money baby." With a big smile on his face.

All Logan could do was shake his head and walk away, and Mrs. Brown continued to help the students get fitted for their caps and gowns.

Logan and Ethan looked around the gym, hopeful that the cool air they felt wasn't Mr. Benjamin Jackson. Mrs. Brown walked over where the they were sitting. "Well boys, next week is going to be your last time here. Aren't you glad that you don't have to put up with Principal Harrison anymore?" When the assistant principal looked at them with a big smile Logan looked at her, then he began to laugh while pulling Ethan to the side.

"What the heck is wrong with our assistant principal, Mrs. Brown? I mean she's really starting to kinda act strange."

Ethan simply looked back at Logan and shrugged his shoulders. "Maybe she's happy, or maybe she feels she doesn't have to worry about Mr. Harrison for the rest of the Year. I mean, now who wouldn't be happy about that?"

Logan put one finger over his lips and began to tap on them. "Maybe you're right, it does feel kinda good without him being around," and with that he began to mock how Mr. Harrison would sound, "Go class son! What are you doing in the hallway without a hall pass?!" Both of the Matthew brothers began to laugh.

Ethan tapped Logan on the shoulder. "Come, so we can get in that line. It's starting to get a little long." As Logan and Ethan got closer to the table to be fitted for their caps and gowns, Logan did began to feel a bit of a cool breeze.

As he turned and looked back at Ethan and used his face to indicate air around and how the temperature was coming down Ethan began to feel that something was wrong. "I mean, I know you are excited and everything, but do you have to look like that?" Logan grinned. As he began to walk up closer to the table, the breeze began to get a little cooler. Logan tried to hurry up, but kept turning back around, however Ethan kept on pushing him forward. "Come on man, will you go ahead, and stop playing."

Logan moved slower and slower. When he reached the table his whole body started to shake. Logan took in a deep breath, and he let out a cool stream of frosty white air.

Ethan studied Logan carefully, then asked, "Hey man, you sure you're Okay?"

As Logan turned around and looked back at his brother her declared, "Yeah, I'm Okay, it's just my nerves trying to act up. You know it is our last time being here." He turned back around and looked at the old man in front of him. Logan's eyes started to widen. "Hello, my name is Logan Matthew. I'm here to be fitted for my cap and gown." Logan's voice had started to tremble when the man lifted his head. It was all Logan could do to swallow the air that was left in his body. He looked the old man up and down, and he noticed that this old man was wearing blue jean overalls with a thin hoodie pulled up over his head.

As the old man raised his head. He looked right at Logan and Ethan. "I told you that this day was not over. Now I have you right where I want you at, and there's no one can stop me. I want my revenge, and I want your souls now.

Ethan jumped in front of Logan, pulled out the name tag and threw it on the table. "Like hell, you will!" The old man disappeared, but smiled as he did so.

A hollow, black, and cloudy voice rang out all over the Gym, "I wanted my Revenge, I wanted your soul! I will continue to hurt you down Logan and Ethan! You will give me your souls! This is not over!" Black shadows and dust that had suddenly filled the air, started to vanish as quickly.

Ethan and Logan looked at one another and nodded with the knowledge that Mr. Benjamin Jackson's soul was still not resting and had turned into a ... Grand Reaper – The Soul Snatcher.

*Linda Spence Howard*

colophon
Brought to you by Wider Perspectives Publishing, care of James Wilson, with the mission of advancing the poetry and creative community of Hampton Roads, Virginia.
See our production of works from ...

Edith Blake
Tanya Cunningham-Jones
     (Scientific Eve)
Terra Leigh
Ray Simmons
Samantha Borders-Shoemaker
Taz Waysweete'
Bobby K.
     (The Poor Man's Poet)
J. Scott Wilson (TEECH!)
Charles Wilson
Gloria Darlene Mann
Neil Spirtas
Zach Crowe
Jorge Mendez & JT Williams
Sarah Eileen Williams
Stephanie Diana (Noftz)
the Hampton Roads
     Artistic Collective
Jason Brown (Drk Mtr)
Martina Champion
Tony Broadway
Ken Sutton
Crickyt J. Expression
Lisa M. Kendrick
Cassandra IsFree
Nich (Nicholis Williams)
Samantha Geovjian Clarke
Natalie Morison-Uzzle
Gus Woodward II
Patsy Bickerstaff
Catherine TL Hodges
Jack Cassada

... and others to come soon.

We promote and support the artists of the 757
*from the seats, from the stands,*
*from the snapping fingers and*
          *clapping hands*
*from the pages, and the stages*
*and now we pass them forth*
          *to the ages*

Check for the above artists on FaceBook, the Virginia Poetry Online channel on YouTube, and other social media.

Hampton Roads Artistic Collective is the non-profit extension of WPP and strives to simultaneously support worthy causes in Hampton Roads and the creative artists.

www.ingramcontent.com/pod-product-compliance
Lightning Source LLC
Chambersburg PA
CBHW050757250626
47155CB00005B/2109